WATERLOO HIGH SCHOOL LIBRARY
1464 INDUSTRY RD.
ATWATER, OHIO 44201

W9-CKH-763

WATERLOO HIGH SCHOOL LIBRARY
1464 INDUSTRY RD.
ATWATER, OHIO 44201

UP AGAINST
THE LAW

WATERLOO HIGH SCHOOL LIBRARY
1464 INDUSTRY RD.
ATWATER OHIO

UP AGAINST THE LAW

YOUR LEGAL RIGHTS AS A MINOR

ROSS R. OLNEY & PATRICIA J. OLNEY

LODESTAR BOOKS   E. P. DUTTON   NEW YORK

347.306
OLN

Copyright © 1985 by Ross R. Olney and Patricia J. Olney

All rights reserved. No part of this publication may be reproduced or transmitted in any form or by any means, electronic or mechanical, including photocopy, recording, or any information storage and retrieval system now known or to be invented, without permission in writing from the publisher, except by a reviewer who wishes to quote brief passages in connection with a review written for inclusion in a magazine, newspaper, or broadcast.

Library of Congress Cataloging in Publication Data

Olney, Ross Robert, date
  Up against the law.

  "Lodestar books."
  Includes index.
  Summary: Discusses the rights and protections extended to minors by the law, the treatment of minors in court, and the responsibility of minors to uphold the law, with many examples of actual and hypothetical cases.
    1. Children—Legal status, laws, etc.—United States— Juvenile literature.   2. Youth—Legal status, laws, etc.— United States—Juvenile literature.   [1. Children— Legal status, laws, etc.   2. Youth—Legal status, laws, etc.   3. Children's rights.   4. Law.   5. Juvenile courts] I. Olney, Patricia J.   II. Title.
KF479.Z9O46   1984   346.7301′35   84-10209
ISBN 0-525-66781-4   347.306′35

Published in the United States by E. P. Dutton, a division of NAL Penguin Inc., 2 Park Avenue, New York, N.Y. 10016

Published simultaneously in Canada by Fitzhenry & Whiteside Limited, Toronto

Editor: Virginia Buckley   Designer: Suzanne Haldane

Printed in the U.S.A.   W
10 9 8 7 6 5 4 3

to those who drafted the United States
Constitution and its amendments,
and to those who have guarded and
defended it since

Contents

1

You Do
Have Rights

You are walking your girl friend home after a school dance
one evening when a gang of several young toughs, guys with
real mean reputations, approaches. They are laughing and having fun. They spot you and your friend and *assault* you. This is a
legal term for name-calling and threatening.

They call you and your girl friend bad names and threaten to
beat you up and rape her. The street is dark and, except for the
two of you and them, deserted. You are enraged and somewhat
frightened at the same time. But you have an ace up your
sleeve. You are the school karate champion, a fact they do not
know. You think you might be able to handle these punks if
push comes to shove. It does, for the leader of the group pokes
you on the shoulder, laughing and making fun of you. He has
committed a *battery* upon you. That is a legal term for touching
you. You decide to take action.

Without further ado, though you still could turn and walk away or at least try to discuss the matter, you chop him across the neck . . . hard! He falls to the sidewalk, and you press your advantage. You jump on him and flail away. You beat him until he is unconscious.

Meanwhile, the others in the gang, awed by your apparent strength, back away and finally flee the scene. Basking in the adoring eyes of your girl friend, you stroll away with her arm in arm. This isn't the Old West, though, and you could be in trouble . . . *serious* trouble!

You could be arrested for battery, for using excessive force; you could even be put in jail. This may not seem right to you, but the law does say you may only use "reasonable force" to resist assault and / or battery.

How about the following situation?

In most states, after midnight, with an intruder in your home, you may not fire a weapon until you have retreated as far as is safely possible. This is the case, even if you are a young woman alone in the house—except for the terrifying intruder! A burglar's life is also precious in the eyes of the law. Although it is true (fortunately) that the district attorney might slide quickly through the investigation about the precise moment you fired the gun, allowing that the intruder should not have been there in the first place, you could be charged with a crime, even murder, if you fire too soon. If you fire too late, it could be too late for you, but that is beside the point of this law.

A stupid law? Possibly, but many more persons than you would ever imagine have been killed because they came home early or unexpectedly.

Here's another situation: Mary is sixteen and pregnant. She is torn between having an abortion or having the baby, but in either case she does not want to name the father. Must she go to her parents? What are her legal rights?

And another: Norman is sixteen years old and wants to leave home. He wants to quit school and work full-time at his job. He has a place to live. He has plans for his future and is unhappy at home. His parents strongly disagree. What are Norman's legal rights?

Finally, this: Arthur was horseplaying with an umbrella. He was jabbing at some friends. The point of the umbrella accidentally struck Thomas in the temple, killing him. Thomas had been objecting to the horseplay. Both boys are minors. What are Arthur's legal rights? What rights do Thomas's survivors have? What will probably happen to Arthur?

In all of this, there is good news and bad news. Times have changed. Not that long ago, you, as a minor, did what you were told to do and didn't ask many questions about it. If your teachers wanted you to do something, you did it—or you failed. You were a teenager, a kid, a student—a nobody—to most adults, at least where "rights" were concerned. You had the rights that anybody allowed you to have and no more.

Any lawyer will tell you that the "law governs us from womb to tomb," from laws on abortion to laws on matters of inheritance. Although times have changed, and you probably have far more rights than you think you have, there are still things in our society that you cannot legally do as a minor.

So here's the bad news. You cannot attend an X-rated movie, you cannot buy intoxicating beverages, and if your parents require it, you must turn over any wages you earn to them.

You may not drive a car until you have reached a certain age, you can be required to attend school, and you must observe any curfew laws in your community.

There are many jobs you cannot take. Serving liquor in a bar, for example, is not a legal job for a minor. You may not marry unless a judge gives permission, and you may not make a legal will.

But here's the good news. More and more, you will find that the laws give minors specific legal rights and protections. You cannot, for example, be held responsible for any contract you make, unless you do so with the idea of cheating somebody. That's why most banks and lending institutions want an adult cosigner on your contracts. You will probably be handled more gently than an adult in a criminal matter and not be punished as severely.

Yes, we live in a free country. But there is no such thing as a right to do anything you wish to do because you are free. It has been said that "your rights stop where the other guy's nose starts." We have laws so that people do not hurt each other. Laws attempt to create a middle ground between freedom and responsibility, between your own rights and the rights of others. Traffic laws protect us. Driver's licenses do the same. You have the right to drive, but you must meet certain restrictions and understand the responsibilities. So must every other driver.

All of us enforce the laws. Not just judges, but everybody. This is true because we choose the people who write the laws and the people who interpret them. And we encourage others to obey the laws by obeying them ourselves.

Try to imagine a hockey game without referees or linesmen. Do you suppose the players—and hockey players are not noted for their good humor or their ability to negotiate calmly— would enforce the rules of the game? They might try, but then somebody would get angry at somebody else, and a pushing match would start. Before long, both teams would be on the ice fighting with each other. This happens even when officials are on the ice, so you can imagine what would happen without them. How about a football game without officials, a baseball game without umpires, or a basketball game without referees? Most of the time, the games would be pandemonium.

That's why we hire policemen. They watch over everybody and see that the laws are obeyed. They may *think* you have broken a law, and they may give you a ticket or even arrest you. But they cannot make the final decision on your alleged breaking of the law. It is up to the courts and the judges and ultimately a jury to make the final decision.

Probably the most important legal document pertaining to your rights is the Constitution of the United States. Our forefathers wanted their sons and daughters and grandchildren and all future generations to live in a free society. But they knew that such a society, to be successful, would need laws. So they wrote a document that gave government certain powers over the people, but reserved most of the rights of freedom to the people themselves. This magnificent document, along with the Bill of Rights, has served our country very well with few changes for over two hundred years.

The Constitution provides for a federal supreme court that eventually hears appeals from all other courts. It is the findings of this court that you will read about in this book, since the decisions of the Supreme Court create precedents that all other courts must follow. The decisions of the Supreme Court are final.

Each state has its own system of laws, though most of them are very similar in nature. You cannot commit murder in any state, for example, but certain states might allow somewhat more latitude in some matters than in others. Each state also has its own state supreme court, as well as courts of appeals.

There are also federal district courts and the federal court of appeals.

Different courts are known by different names in different states. There are superior courts, district courts, small claims courts, probate courts, family courts, county courts, municipal courts, chancery courts, surrogate courts, city courts, traffic courts, and juvenile courts.

There are certain areas of the law that are of special interest to teenagers. Consider these questions, for example:

How long must you go to school?
Must you abide by a school dress code, anywhere, anytime?
When may you get married?
May you obtain birth control devices without your parents' consent?
Are your parents responsible for your actions?
Is it a crime if you "borrow" a car, then return it before you are discovered?
Can you sue someone for making false remarks about you?

Is it a crime to plan a robbery, even if you don't carry it out?

Can you legally punch somebody out for making remarks about your girl friend or boy friend?

Is it a crime to prevent your date from leaving your car if he or she wants to leave it?

What do you do if you owe money?

What if you have been assaulted or battered?

What if you have received a traffic ticket and disagree with the officer?

What if you want to buy a car or a motorcycle?

Learn about your rights in these instances and others. Read on. Enjoy.

2

In School

Young people," said the U.S. Supreme Court in 1975, "do not shed their rights at the schoolhouse door." In fact, the Supreme Court also established the right of students to sue school officials for money damages if their constitutional rights are violated. To sue somebody does not, of course, guarantee that you will collect damages. You must prove your case in a court of law.

Must You Obey a Dress Code?

Let us say that you disagree with your school's dress code. You have decided to protest by wearing clothing of your own choice. The clothing you have decided to wear is reasonable (it covers you adequately). What will happen to you?

You can probably get away with a violation of your school's

dress code without punishment, no matter what your school officials say. But there are some details you should be aware of, and some hazards. You might get the dress code changed, or even thrown out, but you could have to work hard for it. Be sure you feel it will be worth it.

Suppose your school says that jeans are not within the dress-code suggestions. Or, for that matter, neither are T-shirts. The code says that if you are a male student, you must wear slacks and a shirt with a collar. Female students must wear a skirt and a blouse with a collar. Everybody should look neat and tidy. That seems broad enough. Any student should be able to handle guidelines like this.

But along comes a student from a very poor family who cannot afford new clothes. He is from a farm community, and jeans and T-shirts are what he has to wear. The jeans are tattered and the T-shirt is torn.

The school officials cannot insist that the student wear clothing within the dress code. Nor can they suspend him for not complying with the code. The student can wear what he can afford to wear.

Then what about you? If the poor student is permitted to attend class in tattered jeans and a worn T-shirt, why can't you? You can, of course. If the right extends to him, it extends to you as well.

So, does it follow that you can wear anything, regardless of what the dress code says? What about a T-shirt that says THIS SCHOOL SUCKS! There are T-shirts with such slogans, and worse, on some school campuses. If you can wear a T-shirt with a school spirit slogan emblazoned across it, you can probably wear a T-shirt with what some might consider an offensive slogan on it.

How offensive can it be? Many school dress codes are worded to indicate that you cannot wear clothing that might create a "disruption on campus." What if you decided to wear a T-shirt that said SHIT on it? In the law, there are many gray areas. Some persons might insist that such words are or could be disruptive. Others might just laugh the whole thing away.

If you wear such a T-shirt, you must be prepared to face possible suspension or a request that you leave campus and not return until you have changed—at least not until your case is heard and a decision made, and that can take a long time. You must be prepared, if you plan to "fight City Hall," to be told that you do not meet the school's dress code even if the code is not strictly legal.

You may have to give in, go home, and change. Or you can fight for your right to wear what you want to wear. You can make a cause out of it and go all the way to court. This could take years of litigation and a good deal of money unless you can get some lawyer to represent you *pro bono*, for the public good or the welfare of the whole, free. You'll probably win in the long run, but will wearing a T-shirt with a dirty word on it be worth all your trouble? That's where school officials have you with dress codes.

Generally speaking (and unless you are being truly disruptive by wearing a very offensive word), school officials won't want to get involved in a dispute over a dress code. They have learned that dress-code battles are seldom won because the codes are open to such free interpretation. So within reason, you can probably wear what you want to wear.

This all came about because of a particular case. As a result of this case, school officials may still set the rules governing pupil dress, appearance, and behavior, but the rules must be reasonable and have a general public purpose. You can wear almost any type of clothing and cut your hair in generally acceptable ways. Extreme styles in clothing or weird haircuts may still result in suspension, at least until your case is heard. School officials may ban clothing they consider to be immodest, offensive to community standards of good taste, or disruptive. These are all matters of judgment, of course. But remember that courts have generally supported school officials in cases where the student seemed obviously to be going too far.

More about the specific case in a moment.

First, consider the case of a student in Massachusetts who decided to allow his hair to grow to his shoulders in spite of a code that said hair must be cut to a "normal" length. He was the class clown, a real comedian whom everybody liked, and what he was doing was not only by personal choice, it was funny. He liked making the other students smile.

School officials warned him that he would either have to cut his hair or face suspension. He ignored them and took the matter to court. This was in spite of the fact that in one such case, which reached the Massachusetts Supreme Court in 1965, the school officials were upheld. That court held that the student's long hair "could disrupt and impede school decorum."

But times have changed since 1965. Our modern young comedian was allowed to keep his hair at the length he liked. The court said among other things that "within the commodious concept of liberty, embracing freedoms great and small, is the right to wear one's hair as he wishes." This was the meat of the court's findings.

Now for the case that started it all and gave students rights they never had before. It was the famous black armband case, officially known as *Tinker et al.* v. *Des Moines Independent Community School District et al.* (The Latin phrase *et al.* means "and others.")

A ruling was handed down on February 24, 1969, that resulted in new meanings for students according to the First Amendment to the Constitution of the United States. This is the amendment that includes the words, "Congress shall make no laws . . . abridging the freedom of speech. . . ."

Three young people in Des Moines—John Tinker, fifteen; Mary Beth Tinker, thirteen; and Christopher Eckhardt, fifteen—belonged to families who opposed the participation of the United States in the Vietnam War. They were nonviolent protesters, so they decided to oppose the war by wearing black armbands during a "mourning" period from December 16 until New Year's Day.

Meanwhile, a student from a Des Moines high school was forbidden to write an article on the war for the school newspaper. A meeting of school principals resulted in a vote not to allow the article because the subject was too controversial. At the same meeting, the principals voted not to allow the students to wear black armbands to protest the war. That's how things were then.

No! said the families involved. On December 16, as planned, the three students wore their black armbands at their three separate schools. (Two elementary school students, Paul Tinker and Hope Tinker, also wore black armbands, but they were not a part of the subsequent legal actions.)

"Remove them!" was the order from school officials.

The three students refused and were sent home with instructions to return only when the armbands were gone. They didn't return until their self-imposed mourning period had ended, following the holiday vacation. This, perhaps, could have ended the case. But it didn't. The Tinkers felt that their right to free speech and self-expression had been violated. They went to court, and the Iowa Civil Liberties Union agreed to help them.

What followed was a good example of the old argument between the duty of school officials to maintain order and the rights of students to the protections offered by the Constitution of the United States.

In the first round, the U.S. district court held that the school officials had been right. "The avowed purpose of the plaintiffs [the Tinkers] in this instance was to express their views on a controversial subject . . . [and] while the armbands themselves may not be disruptive, the reactions and comments from other students as a result of the armbands would be likely to disturb the disciplined atmosphere required for any classroom." Thus, ruled the court, the school officials had the right to restrict this type of protest.

So the Iowa Civil Liberties Union carried the case to the U.S. Court of Appeals in the Eighth Circuit. The eight justices were evenly divided, and the decision was allowed to stand.

The U.S. Supreme Court was petitioned by the Civil Liberties Union and agreed to hear the case. Almost four years after the students had worn their black armbands, the decision was announced. By a vote of seven to two, the lower court's ruling was reversed. The U.S. Supreme Court ruled that the Des Moines school officials had denied the petitioners their rights under the First Amendment.

The high court's decision had solidly affirmed the civil rights of students. Young people, indeed, do not shed their rights at the schoolhouse door.

One school system totally stripped down the dress code for their schools. Beards would be allowed, as well as blue jeans for girls and many other clothing and grooming habits that were formerly banned. Dress and grooming that met the criteria for "cleanliness, health, safety, and decency" would be permitted.

How about bare feet? No, since a barefoot student in the metal shop or other school areas would be facing a definite safety hazard. How long could hair be? As long as the wearer wanted it to be, though it had to be clean and it had to be safe. For example, a student working around machines of any type would have to cut his or her hair short or roll it into a net. This type of dress code is becoming more and more popular in schools around the country. Reasonable? Probably so.

Three students in another public school system, however, were recently refused admission to their school because they declined to shave off their beards. The case went to court. Can you guess what happened?

Surely the students were allowed to keep their beards in this modern day of freedom of choice? No. An appellate court found that the rule against beards in school was reasonable. They held that the rule had a proper public purpose. They found that the rule was to keep out of the school anybody whose appearance would distract others from their studies. However, the Supreme Court may rule in favor of the students eventually, if the case is appealed to that level.

Be careful when you are exercising your First Amendment rights in school. They can be tricky. You must be on solid ground, even today.

Is a Locker Search Legal?

The Fourth Amendment to the Constitution of the United States affirms the right of the people "to be secure in their persons, houses, papers and effects, against unreasonable searches." Clear enough, you might say. You cannot be searched unreasonably, nor can your house, papers, or other effects be searched unreasonably. The Constitution of the United States guarantees that.

What about your locker at school? Once again you will find yourself in a gray area. That word *unreasonable* is the thorn. What is reasonable and what is not, and who decides?

One high school student is known to be a seller of pills. Another student tells the principal. The principal, without a search warrant, or permission from the student, or anything else, goes directly to the "pusher's" locker and opens it. Inside he finds no pills, but a stash of marijuana.

The student is quickly found guilty of violating the state's Health and Safety Code. But he appeals. He says that the search was illegal, that no warrant had been issued nor permission given. Therefore, the marijuana evidence should not have been admitted in court. And without the marijuana, there was no case. He wanted the conviction overturned.

Appeal denied. Conviction affirmed. The search was held to be reasonable and legal, under the circumstances.

Don't put anything in your school locker, especially in high school (laws are somewhat more vague in colleges) that you don't want found. Generally speaking, nobody has the right to search your locker without a warrant, but there are exceptions. And often those exceptions are in the eyes of the searcher.

Alcohol and other drugs are now widespread in schools. Violence is increasing. So serious discussions have been held about allowing a search of a student's body, locker, and possessions. The courts have generally taken a middle-of-the-road position. School officials may not routinely search a locker, nor may a school official, on the basis of vague suspicion, demand that a student open a locker or dump the contents of pocket or purse. But if there is evidence that the student might be hiding something that is illegal, then the school official is within his or her right to search.

Who decides whether or not there is evidence? The school official does, so be careful.

Prayer in School

One teacher in a Bible Belt school decided to begin her daily class with everybody saying the Lord's Prayer. Not only that, but she insisted all the students take part. This was not in 1949 but in 1979! One student declined to participate, and the teacher asked that student to leave the room while the prayer was in progress. The student objected and was sent home.

The teacher was not familiar with the 1963 finding of the U.S. Supreme Court in the *Abington School District* v. *Schempp* case. Abington High School, in suburban Philadelphia, began the school day with a religious exercise over the public address system. A few verses from the Bible would be read, then the students in all the homerooms would rise to repeat the Lord's Prayer. The practice was, at that time, required by Pennsylvania law, which said that at least ten verses of the Bible were to be read, without comment, at the beginning of each school day.

Ellory Schempp, a junior, refused to attend this required devotional period. He and his family were members of a religious group that rejected the idea that Jesus was the son of God. Schempp insisted that he should not be forced to listen to these verses, which contained ideas he rejected, such as the divinity of Christ.

By a vote of eight to one, the Supreme Court held that the Pennsylvania law on reading the Bible was inconsistent with the establishment clause of the First Amendment. Justice Tom Clark, in the majority opinion, concluded that the Constitution imposes a duty of "neutrality" upon the government where religion is concerned. At the same time, the Court was hearing a similar case based on a Bible reading law in Maryland.

The majority opinion was that such procedures violated the separation of church and state. It said that this separation must be absolute and must be strictly and fiercely enforced.

In the flowery language of law, the Court found that "It is no defense to urge that the religious practices here may be relatively minor encroachments on the First Amendment. The breach of neutrality that is today a trickling stream may all too soon become a raging torrent."

But couldn't the students who disagreed merely leave the room? Wouldn't that protect their rights?

No, said the Supreme Court. Such students might be deterred from seeking to be excused for fear of being held up to public scorn or being branded as "oddballs."

Schools may observe a moment of silence for individual prayer or meditation, since the decision of the Court did not specifically discuss this practice. Also, of course, schools may objectively study the Bible and the history of religion and its place in the advancement of civilization. Students may also be excused from school to go and participate in religious ceremonies or services, but a teacher may not bring religion into the classroom in the form of recitation or prayers.

Are religious exercises outlawed in public schools in all fifty states? Yes. There should be no prayer in your classroom even though some have suggested that since most students and parents approve of prayer, the law against these exercises could be a violation of the civil rights of the majority.

Another question was raised in the case. What about the words *under God* in the pledge of allegiance recited by all students and many public officials in public forums? Isn't this a violation of the separation of church and state?

No, said a concurring opinion to the majority decision. Associate Justice William J. Brennan, Jr., wrote that the pledge will probably not be changed because the reciting of it is not a "religious exercise," but rather a recognition of "the historical fact that our nation was believed to have been founded 'under God.'"

Must You Go to School?

A student in California by the name of Bill Miller is six feet, two inches tall and weighs more than two hundred pounds. He has a beard and looks more like a teacher than a student. He looks much older than his fifteen years. He is bored with school and has nothing in common with his classmates, who look at him as some sort of freak.

All Bill wants to do is quit school and join the navy. That has been his lifelong dream. He is sure he will be accepted in the navy and will be happy to be with people his own size.

He even fooled the navy by lying about his age, but they discovered his true age and sent him home. Must he return to the tenth grade and face his young classmates again?

California's laws are much like those in most states. Miller has little choice. He must return to public school unless he is "exempted." Every person from six to sixteen must attend school full-time. You can be exempted in California and most other states for any of the following reasons:

1. You are going to private day school full-time and are taught by persons capable of teaching.
2. You have a physical or mental condition that prevents school attendance or renders it inadvisable.
3. You are mentally gifted and are instructed in a full-time day school where as much as 50 percent of the instructional time may be taught in a foreign language.
4. You are being taught by a private tutor with valid credentials.
5. You are blind or deaf, and no schools for the blind or deaf are available in your area.

There are alternatives in Miller's case, such as the school principal recommending that he be assigned to a vocational school or a special school where the emphasis is on instruction with an occupation in mind. But generally speaking, he must return to school, as unpleasant as that thought might be to Bill. He might be able to arrange a combination work-school schedule or some other specially designed program, but he must be instructed.

Bus Behavior Is Important

Claude and Marty were buddies and the clowns of Bus 14. Every morning the other students looked forward to the stop where Claude and Marty got on. From that moment on, hilarity broke loose. If Claude wasn't acting foolish, Marty was. Both boys, it seemed, would do anything for a laugh.

One morning, in fact, they began marching up and down the aisle, goose-stepping and showing off. Everybody was laughing and it was all in good fun. But the driver, Mr. Perkins, repeatedly told them to sit down. Finally Mr. Perkins reached the end of his patience. He turned around and shouted, "Down, boys. Sit *down!*"

At that instant the bus was moving through an intersection. Little Joey Adams, in a crosswalk with his mother on the way to another school, was struck and killed by the bus. Suddenly the humor of Claude and Marty didn't seem very funny anymore. Mr. Perkins was beside himself with grief and worry.

And what about the contribution of Claude and Marty to the tragedy? Both boys are in very serious trouble. They probably will be sued for the wrongful death of Joey.

But wait a minute. Wasn't this an accident, pure and simple? A tragedy, yes, but still just an accident? Doesn't everybody know that some accidents are unavoidable?

In this case, though, Claude and Marty continued to act up even after the driver, Mr. Perkins, had warned them. They were endangering pedestrians and the other students on the bus.

3

Family
and Home

Remember Mary from the first chapter? She is sixteen and pregnant. She is torn between having an abortion or having the baby, but in either case does not want to name the father. What are her legal rights?

Very wisely, Mary consulted a counselor at school. She explained to the sympathetic woman that the father of the baby was not her real concern. She was torn, she said, between the substantial interference a pregnancy would create in her life and normal routine and how it might disturb her future plans, and how an abortion might affect her now and later. And if she had the baby, what would she do with it? She was a tenth grader and her parents were antagonistic and hostile about the entire situation. She knew she could put the baby up for adoption, of course, but was not sure that was what she really wanted.

The counselor pointed out that many agencies and individuals hoping to adopt children would cooperate with care and expenses during her pregnancy and hospital stay. But the counselor also reaffirmed Mary's fears about what the term of pregnancy would do to her life as a high school student. She'd made a mistake, yes, but there was still time to have an abortion and then allow the matter to fade.

Mary's decision was to have the abortion. And, yes, even though she is a minor and not married, she has a right to get an abortion without the consent of her partner or that of a judge. Most important to Mary, the consent of her parents was not required.

The U.S. Supreme Court held in 1979 that a Massachusetts law requiring minors to get permission from their parents for an abortion was unconstitutional. Nor does a minor need permission from a court. The Supreme Court said that a state *may* require a pregnant minor "to obtain one or both parents' consent to an abortion." But then the Court continued that the state must also provide an alternative procedure whereby authorization for an abortion may be obtained without parental permission. This alternative procedure includes the following.

A pregnant minor may obtain an abortion if (a) she can show that she is mature enough to make such a decision, in consultation with her doctor, even if the decision is contrary to her parents' wishes, or (b) even though she is unable to make this decision independently, the desired abortion can be shown to be in her best interest.

The Supreme Court also upheld an earlier 1976 decision that held that neither parents nor any third party (the father?) has absolute veto, or arbitrary veto, over the decision of the physician and his patient to terminate a patient's pregnancy.

Mary can get her abortion if she wishes, but the Court does not give every minor the absolute right of an adult to an abortion. The Court still feels that children cannot have the same rights as adults because of the vulnerability of children, their possible inability to make critical decisions in a mature manner, and the importance of parental guidance. There is also the need of children for concern, sympathy, and parental attention.

Note that although Mary can get an abortion without her parents' consent, her parents do know about her condition. You may not need your parents' OK either, but they may be told of your situation and what you are going through if the operation is being done by a legitimate agency or a responsible private doctor.

Further, even now bills are passing through Congress at the same time that the Supreme Court is hearing new arguments on whether or not any woman, minor or adult, should have more control over her reproductive organs than the government has. We should be able to bet on freedom of individual choice, but, on the other hand, government has often tended to meddle into areas of individual morality, or what it considers to be morality, so keep a watch on these matters.

Are Your Parents Responsible for Your Actions?

It was early one morning in 1965, in St. Louis, Missouri. The pleasant residential neighborhood was quiet, with everybody sleeping soundly. Everybody but the milkman, that is, who was making his rounds. He parked his truck to deliver some milk. He left the engine idling, but firmly set the parking brake.

Meanwhile, a three-year-old, awakened perhaps by the sound of the milk bottles, crawled from his bed, walked down the hall past his sleeping parents, and went outside. He climbed into the cab of the milk truck and somehow managed to release the emergency brake. The truck rolled faster and faster down the neighborhood street and finally slammed into a porch, doing considerable damage. Fortunately, the youngster was not injured.

Of course, the distraught parents knew that the neighbor with the smashed porch and the milk company with the battered truck would not be happy about the accident, but they were stunned when they were slapped with a heavy lawsuit from both those parties. They learned that in many cases, parents can be hauled into court for the actions of their minor children.

It is almost impossible to predict the outcome of such lawsuits. Consider the case of a boy who was involved in a fistfight with another boy. The second boy lost two front teeth in the battle. The parents of the first boy were worried that they would be sued, and, in fact, they could be. In such a suit, the court would try to decide which boy was the aggressor and which one was only trying to defend himself. It is possible that the first boy was only using reasonable force to defend himself, and this would weigh heavily in any lawsuit.

There was the case in Florida where a young girl intentionally slammed a door on a hotel employee, seriously injuring the employee's hand.

The key to all three of these cases is the legal term *prior notice*. If the parents are aware that their child has previously harmed someone or damaged somebody's property, this is enough to establish prior notice. The court will then want to know if the parents have made some effort to restrain the minor so that these situations do not occur again.

In all three of the preceding cases, the parents were not held liable because in all three this prior notice was not proven. The little boy who drove the milk truck had never been shown how to release a brake. He had never, according to the court records, released a truck brake before. He *was* shown to have crawled out of windows before; he even had a habit of crawling down manholes. Still, because he had never before released a truck brake, prior notice was not established and the parents were not held liable.

The same was true for the boy who broke the other boy's teeth and the girl who slammed the hotel door. It is very important to the court whether or not children have done damage before, and whether or not the parents have tried to stop them from doing damage.

One parent allowed his child to continue to use an air rifle even though the youngster had shot at birds, windows, and other children before. Finally the child injured another child seriously with a shot from his gun. The court refused to dismiss the case against the parents because they *knew* their child could be dangerous to others. They had to agree, finally, to an out-of-court settlement for a substantial sum of money.

Another boy shot a neighbor in the eye with a slingshot his mother had given to him. No liability, a court decided later, since the boy had not been known to shoot at people. It was an accident, pure and simple.

Generally speaking, your parents can be held liable for something you do as a minor if you can be shown to have done something like it in the past. On the other hand, if you do something you might not be expected to do, they may not be held liable for your action. They will, however, be held *more* liable if what you have done involves a motor vehicle. Your parents have, in many states, given tacit permission for you to drive by signing your driver's license application, and the court knows this.

Finally, nobody ever knows what a jury is going to do in these cases. They may find for you or for the other side, and their word, not the judge's (in most cases), is final. So be careful.

Who Gets Your Paycheck?

Young Johnny screamed loudly when his parents asked for his first paycheck from his new job at a fast-food store. But scream as he may, Johnny has a problem. He is not yet *emancipated.*

Minors become emancipated when they become adults. At that time, they are legally able to take full charge of their lives. Also they can assume legal responsibility for their own support and their own actions. In some states, minors can become emancipated by marrying or by a legal agreement with their parents. The parents must agree that the children are old enough to support themselves.

An emancipated minor may claim his own earnings, but Johnny cannot. He lives at home without paying room and board. He is under the supervision of his parents. Even though he is paying for his own clothes, perhaps, or his own car and stereo set, and other expenses, he still must hand over his paycheck to his parents if they request it. That's the law.

Internationally famous as a child motion-picture star, Jackie Coogan earned more than $7 million dollars. He played "The Kid" with Charlie Chaplin and in other movies. He was very popular and very successful.

His natural mother and stepfather kept the bulk of his money, so he finally sued them. But he only collected about $200,000; and after legal fees, he netted only about $30,000. In order to solve the kind of problem that arose in Coogan's case, the California legislature did enact a law under which 50 percent of the net earnings of a child athlete or actor or creative artist must be retained for the child in a trust fund under a court-approved contract. This money is then transferred to the child when he reaches majority.

Who May Marry?

But let's say Johnny is really unhappy. Not only does he resist handing over his paycheck to his parents but he knows that by marrying he will be emancipated. Mumbling that he is nothing more than a slave, he suggests to Mary Ann, his girl friend, that they marry. Both of them, he points out, will then be free to run their own lives.

This isn't going to be as easy as he thinks. In fact, minors who marry without parental consent, when it is required in their state, are not even legally married. Parents can go to court and get the marriage ended, a process called *annulment.*

But Johnny has an idea. He and Mary Ann cross the state line to a state where marriage laws are much less strict. In the neighboring state, parental consent is not required for minors to

WATERLOO HIGH SCHOOL LIBRARY
1464 INDUSTRY RD.
ATWATER, OHIO 44201

be legally married. In Alabama, for example, the legal age for marriage without parental consent is fourteen for girls and seventeen for boys. Since Johnny is seventeen and Mary Ann sixteen, they could be married in Alabama without any trouble. In Colorado, the age for marriage without parental consent is eighteen for girls and twenty-one for boys. It wouldn't do Johnny and Mary Ann much good to go to Colorado. California, in an effort to recognize the equality of men and women, set the age at eighteen for both males and females to marry without parental consent. And in California, boys and girls under eighteen can marry with the consent of their parents and the authorization of a superior court judge.

So Johnny and Mary Ann go to Alabama and get married. Then they hurry back home, secure in the knowledge that they have legally married and nobody, including parents, can undo what the state of Alabama has done.

Wrong. If they had stayed in Alabama they would have been all right. But by returning home, they made it obvious that they only used the laws of the state of Alabama to circumvent the laws of their own state. That won't work. The parents got the courts of their home state to deny the legality of the marriage.

So Johnny had to hand over his paycheck anyway. He could have saved a lot of trouble and unhappiness if he had done it in the first place.

What Is Marriage?

Johnny didn't understand that marriage is much more than being together, sleeping in the same bed, caring for each other and wanting to spend two lives together.

Certain specific moral responsibilities and duties are created by the marriage ceremony, which is also a legal ceremony that creates a contract between the husband and the wife. In this ceremony, both parties agree before witnesses to take on certain obligations. They agree that they owe each other mutual obligations of love, faithfulness, confidence, comfort, sympathy, support, respect, honesty, understanding, and integrity.

More and more, marriage means mutuality. Marriage means equality. What the wife owes her husband, he owes her. The two partners are equal, and neither promises more than the other.

Marriage is serious—a lifelong commitment—and should be approached for its own sake, not as a tool for some other purpose as Johnny and Mary Ann tried to make it.

Annulment Can Happen

An annulment is the erasure of a marriage by a court order. The order ends the marriage as though it never existed. That is the difference between an annulment and a divorce. With a divorce, you were married, but now you are not. You have an ex-husband or ex-wife.

With an annulment, legally speaking, you were never married in the first place.

The grounds for annulment have nothing specifically to do with whether or not the parties have consummated the marriage (had sex with each other), though state laws do vary. Certainly if either party was under the influence of drugs or alcohol and did not realize what was happening, grounds are established. Also, if either party was below the age of consent or married without parental or court permission, the marriage can be annulled. Other grounds for annulment vary, depending on different state laws.

Birth Control Devices

Glenda has fallen in love with Harold. She can't seem to concentrate or to take her eyes off him during the eleventh grade class they share. Harold returns the affection, but there is a complication. He wants to have sex "just like everybody else."

That, according to Harold, is the way people who are in love with each other show their feelings.

Furthermore, Harold is quick with statistics. He knows that a 1976 study by some professors from a major university showed that 63.3 percent of American teenage girls had sexual intercourse before marriage, and one in ten became pregnant before the age of seventeen. Harold knows what everybody else knows, that sexual mores have changed, and this has led to more sexual intercourse between young unmarried persons.

New York State, where Glenda and Harold live, had made it illegal for anyone to furnish contraceptive devices to minors. It was felt this would discourage promiscuous sexual activity among the young. But under all the pressure, Glenda finally decided to give in. Without telling her parents, she went to a family planning center to ask for a contraceptive. Between Harold's pressuring and the fact that many of her peers were having relations and making no effort to hide it, she wanted to join the group. And she didn't want to tell her parents. They wouldn't understand her love for Harold.

Would she be able to obtain contraception and would the agency deal only with her and not tell her parents? Probably.

The U.S. Supreme Court held in 1977 that the New York State law was unconstitutional. The high court based the decision on the right to privacy afforded by the due process clause of the Fourteenth Amendment. Whether you are married or single, the court determined, you have a right to be free of unwarranted governmental intrusion in the area of personal decisions regarding contraception. The government, in other words, has no right to influence you one way or the other. In a sense, they said, the law would be telling you whether or not you could or should have a child.

The Supreme Court also doubted that withholding contraceptive devices would cut down on sex between young people. Probably the sex would continue, but more girls would become pregnant. Most family planning experts agree. They feel that the best way is to allow the matter of sex to be a personal decision, and meanwhile to make available devices to prevent pregnancy among those who have decided to go ahead.

But wait a minute. This matter has come up again, and now the courts are looking at whether or not a minor should be allowed to obtain birth control devices without parental knowledge. The legality of the so-called squeal law (requiring parents to be told if minors ask for birth control devices) is still being argued; so keep an eye on the matter.

What Is a Minor?

With all this talk of minors, when does minority end? The Twenty-sixth Amendment to the U.S. Constitution, adopted in 1971, says: "The right of citizens of the United States, who are eighteen years of age or older, to vote shall not be denied or abridged by the United States or by any state on account of age."

Great! People thought this new right would satisfy the protesters who marched and preached about making young men—who couldn't even vote for the leaders who were sending them—go off to fight wars. It would satisfy the students who insisted that if the right to vote were given to younger people, the world would improve. It would once and for all end the strife and tension that prevailed in our land at that time.

States generally proceeded to extend all rights and duties of adulthood to eighteen-year-olds, with some exceptions. Many states resisted allowing eighteen-year-olds to drink or buy alcoholic beverages. Some states allowed eighteen-year-olds to drink beer and wine, but not harder liquors. One state, Oklahoma, decided to allow females to buy 3.2 beer (with less alcohol) at age eighteen, but to withhold the same right from males until they are twenty-one. The U.S. Supreme Court struck that down as denying equal rights to males.

Unfortunately, the participation of these new voters in the democratic process didn't change things very much. Many of the protesters who were shouting for the right to vote then have become protesters shouting down the rights of others to speak now. And, generally, the same percentage of citizens who always voted are still voting. In 1976, long enough for the Twenty-sixth Amendment to have taken effect, 54.3 percent of the voting age population (including new eighteen-year-olds) cast ballots in the presidential election. In 1978 only 35.2 percent of those who could vote, did, though this was an "off-year" election. The next presidential election, in 1980, was no improvement over 1976. Only 53.9 percent of voting age people actually took the trouble to vote.

As always, a majority of a solid minority continues to make the laws for all of us by taking the trouble to vote for the lawmakers.

Some states, at first Illinois and Michigan, began to revert to age twenty-one for drinking. Due to an alarming increase in alcohol involving auto accidents, other states also reconsidered. Maine and Massachusetts raised the drinking age to twenty. You can find out what the age of drinking is in your state by calling any local city hall, politician, police department, or elected official.

Of course, the right to vote does not necessarily carry with it the right to all other majority (legal adulthood) rights. Drinking is just one right that states still control. The right to marry, to make contracts, to be tried as an adult (or minor), and other legal responsibilities covered in other chapters of this book are still often determined by your state. The age for majority is still twenty-one in common law and remains so in many states, even though many others have lowered the legal age for certain activities.

4

Contracts

Harry looks much older than his seventeen years. He walks into Fast Eddie's Used-Car Lot and talks Eddie into selling him a car. The two make up the contract, and Harry pays Eddie the down payment. Then Harry drives away in the car.

But on the way home, he sails through a stop sign and in an effort to avoid other cars he runs smack into a huge tree. Harry is only shaken up, but the car is severely damaged. Harry looks over the car and decides that, among other things, he didn't really like the color anyhow. Furthermore, now that he thinks about it, he really wanted a sports car, not a sedan.

So Harry calls Fast Eddie and tells him that he is no longer interested in the car. He tells Eddie that he is only seventeen years old and that the contract they have signed isn't worth the paper it is written on. Not that Harry intended to defraud Eddie. He really thought he wanted the car. But he doesn't want it anymore, so he tells Eddie to come and get it. And he'd better bring a flatbed truck, Harry tells Eddie, recalling the smoking ruins still waiting on the corner of Main and Elm.

Eddie is very angry and decides he isn't going to stand for this. The used-car business is tough enough without this sort of thing happening. He won't get taken this way!

But he probably will. There isn't much Fast Eddie can do in this situation. It does no good for a merchant to claim that he thought the purchaser of merchandise was an adult. And minors, as most merchants know, cannot be held responsible for many contracts they make. Minors are assumed by the law to lack the judgment that most adults are supposed to have.

In Harry's case, the courts, if Fast Eddie actually wants to take it that far, will probably tell Eddie to pay back the money Harry gave him. They might allow Eddie to keep enough money to make up for losses due to the damage done to the car, but this isn't always the case. Most states will also require the minor to return anything he gained from the bargain that is still in his possession. In this case, Harry would have to give back the remains of the car.

Ultimately, Fast Eddie went to a lawyer to initiate a lawsuit against Harry's parents for the value of the car Harry bought and then wrecked. Eddie felt that the parents should be responsible for a contract made by their minor child.

Again Eddie had no luck. Harry's parents had not cosigned the papers, agreeing ahead of time to be responsible for the loan, so they are not involved in the situation. Parents are not generally responsible for the contracts of their minor children.

What Is a Contract?

A contract is an agreement between two or more parties, each of whom gives something, promises something, or does something (or promises *not* to do something) as his or her part of the agreement. If you purchase a pair of pants and charge it, you are giving your promise to pay and the merchant is giving you the pants.

If you agree to mow your neighbor's lawn for a fee and the neighbor agrees to the fee, you have made a contract with him. Then you mow the lawn as your part of the agreement, and he pays you the money as his part.

Sometimes one party does not live up to the contract's terms and promises. You might mow the lawn and then your neighbor might refuse to pay you. This is a *breach of contract.*

The difference between you breaching a contract and an adult breaching a contract is substantial. A breach of contract by an adult caused by a failure to live up to the terms of the agreement (even to not paying for a lawn-mowing job) may lead to a lawsuit by the other party to the contract. That party may sue for money damages or to compel the first party to live up to the terms of the agreement.

With minors, though, most such agreements are voidable. Even within a reasonable time after the minor has become an adult, he or she may cancel an agreement made before adulthood without penalty. If the minor has any money or other valuables as a result of the contract, they might have to be returned, but if there is nothing (such as in the case of the wrecked car), the minor can still get any money back that has been paid without having to return anything (at least not anything but junk).

And here's a little more good news. If a minor makes an agreement with an adult, such as mowing the lawn, and the *adult* breaches the agreement, the adult can be sued by the minor. Just because you can't be held to a contract doesn't mean that adults do not have to live up to the terms of a contract they have made with you. Still, it isn't all roses in this area. Don't ever try to use this right to *defraud.*

There was the case of William, who posed as his older brother, Stanley, to buy a used car. He used his older brother's driver's license as identification and bought a sleek sports car. The dealer, Honest Dave, had no reason to suspect anything and was quite happy to make the deal with "Stanley."

William gave Dave $600 on the car as a down payment and agreed to pay off the remaining $5,000 plus interest and carrying charges over the next two years. Everybody shook hands, the deal was made, and William drove away.

But soon William grew tired of the car. It was running fine, but it wasn't what he really wanted. He drove it back to Dave's used-car lot and parked it. Then he asked for his deposit back. Dave pointed out that William had used the car, that he couldn't return it right after buying it. "Nonsense," said William-posing-as-Stanley, thinking he was wise to the ways of the law. Then he dropped his bombshell, his ace in the hole, or so he thought. He pointed out that he was a minor and could not be held to a contract.

But Dave was no fool and no stranger to the law either. He knew that his particular state bars a minor from voiding a contract such as this one. In this case, he might force William to keep the car because William *intended* to defraud him. Generally speaking, though, Dave would probably get stuck with the car and he would probably have to return all of William's money, too. In spite of the fact that William had actually committed fraud by using his brother's driver's license, he is probably in the clear. Adults cannot sue minors for things such as this in *many* states. But be aware that this law is changing in some states, so don't test it. Honesty would forbid such a test anyhow.

On the other hand, suppose William loved the car, took care of it, drove it with pleasure, and paid off the loan according to the contract. No further action is taken or necessary. The agreement itself, remember, is not illegal or immoral. It is simply unenforceable if one of the parties is a minor who decides to avoid the obligations specified in the contract.

But this is not always true. Although there are certain contracts which, if made by a minor, are void—have no legal effect—(a cosigning of another's loan, for example, or a contract to sell real estate or one to give a power of attorney to another person), there are certain other contracts that are legal and binding even when made by a minor.

A contract for enlistment into the armed forces, for example, is legal and binding. Be sure you want to when you sign those papers, because even though you are under twenty-one, you are bound by the contract you have made. There may be other ways to get out of it, but merely walking away, as you can do in many other contractual matters, will not work.

A contract for a student loan is also legal and binding, and so is a contract for life insurance or for necessary medical care. Remember Mary, who wanted the abortion? She is going to have to sign some contractual papers at the clinic where she is having her operation. Those papers are legal, and she is legally old enough to sign them.

Minors are responsible for the reasonable value or fair price, appropriate to their "station in life," of certain *quasi-contracts* (as they are known in the law). If the minor is living alone, necessities not furnished by one's parents might be an example—food, clothing, medical supplies, shelter, education, and the like. The minor would be held responsible for payments for such necessities contracted by them.

Written or Oral Contracts

Certain contracts must be in writing according to the laws of individual states. In most states a contract for the purchase of real estate must be in writing to be enforceable by the courts. In Florida, a magazine subscription, which is a contract, must be in writing.

If state law requires a contract to be written, and it is not written but only agreed to orally, it is not enforceable in court.

Remember, even as a minor you can make a contract where a contract is required, but it usually must be cosigned by an adult. The adult will have the final responsibility if you decide to breach the agreement. But also remember that if the other party is an adult, he or she must abide by the terms of the contract even though you are a minor.

What About an Illegal Contract?

Greedy Grody owned a junkyard. He knew that copper cable was valuable. He could sell it by the pound at a high price. Along came Donald Dumbhead asking for a job. Grody made an oral contract with Donald. He pointed out a nearby housing development where there were stacks of copper cable. All Donald had to do, said Grody, was steal some cable, bring it to the junkyard, and Grody would buy it from him.

Donald could make some quick money he needed, Grody could make a profit selling the cable to his sources, and the loss to the developer would be paid for by an insurance company. Everybody would be happy—except the insurance company— and Grody quickly assured Donald that insurance companies have so much money that they don't really mind claims as small as this one was going to be.

What Dumbhead needs to know, besides the obvious, is that Grody does not have to buy the copper after Donald has stolen it. A contract such as this is illegal. And if Donald decides to sue (well, we said he was a dumbhead), Grody can defend himself successfully by proving that the purpose of the contract was illegal.

Minors Are Treated Differently in Contracts

In all states, minors are treated differently in contract matters. If you are going to make mistakes, and everybody does, it will probably be when you are younger and have less experience. The law recognizes this fact. It also recognizes that people with experience can, and have been known to, take advantage of younger people. So the law will not permit an adult to take unfair advantage of a minor. Under most circumstances, the law will permit a minor to void a contract he or she does not wish to be in.

Remember this, though. William, who took advantage of

Honest Dave, may not be completely safe. There are a few states, among them Washington, Michigan, and Utah, where a minor who has made a contract by lying about his age can be held responsible for it.

The laws protecting minors from adults who might try to cheat them are to help an inexperienced minor facing an experienced adult. If the matter is turned around, and a minor is trying to cheat an adult (e.g., what William was trying to do to Dave), the law sometimes works the other way. Don't go around making contracts you don't intend to keep, for the purpose of cheating somebody. Don't abuse this protection the law gives you.

Checks, Rubber and Otherwise

You know that you can sign the back of your own paycheck and cash it at the bank even though you are a minor. You can even have a checking account, in spite of the law that allows minors to disallow their contracts.

It would be illegal, in other words, to write a bad check just because you are a minor and not responsible for your contracts. Nor can you cash a check from somebody else when you know that there are insufficient funds in the check writer's account.

A check is a negotiable instrument and, in a sense, a contract. Almost like cash, it is a promise to pay and can be transferred from one person to another by a signature on the back. If you sell a bicycle to Stan and he gives you a check in payment, it is in many ways as though he is giving you cash. He is promising you that he has enough money in his account at the bank to cover the amount he owes you. As a result, he is giving you a written instrument that you can exchange for money.

You may not want to take it to his bank. You may want to deposit it in your own account in your bank, or you may want to cash it at the local store. Since it is like cash, your bank will accept it into your account. Some stores will also cash it, although many stores do not like to take checks that are not made out to the store itself. The store calls these *second party* checks.

Suppose Stan is careless about his promises. Suppose he really doesn't have money in his account at the bank. Are you responsible?

Yes—if you *knew* he didn't have the money in his account. You are just as wrong to take his check and try to cash it, with the knowledge that there is no money in the account, as Stan was in writing the bad check in the first place.

But let's assume that you didn't know. Then your bank or your store will send the check back to you, marked Insufficient Funds. And you will have to go back to Stan and try to get your money. You can do this by asking for it or by arranging to go to small-claims court.

If you endorse a check from Stan and then spend it as cash at a store (or deposit it in your bank), you are making certain guarantees with your signature. You are making a legal promise that the check belongs to you, that you have the legal right to endorse it, that it is a good check (to your best knowledge) with money backing it in the bank, and that you will pay the cash to the store or bank if the check is refused by Stan's bank.

You do have a right here that you may not be aware of. As in the case of most contracts made by minors, if the check you received from Stan and paid to the store for merchandise bounces, the store cannot *sue* you for payment. But you must exercise your right as a minor to disclaim liability. You must state to the store that you are a minor and are not responsible for the check.

Remember, though, this is only in the case of a check you assumed to be good. If you knew Stan's check was rubber, then you would lose the right to disclaim liability for passing it on. You are committing a crime, and for this you will be held responsible.

The fact is, the system of banking that we have in this country is based upon good faith. Certainly many people, adults and minors, take advantage of it; but as a general rule, it works because the vast majority of people who use it do so honestly.

5

Some Protections and Freedoms

You and your boy friend are driving along on a fine sunny day. You have prepared a basket with sandwiches and cool drinks, it waits in the back seat, and you are both getting hungry. Ah, there's a nice, cool-looking spot just off the road. You pull over, unload the food, spread a blanket, and relax.

You both ignore the prominent NO TRESPASSING sign on a tree near where you are resting.

Real Property

Just as you are getting comfortable, the sheriff comes along, gives you a ticket, and tells you that the fine can be substantial. You are shocked since you did nothing to harm anything or anybody.

But an owner does have the right to keep people off his property for whatever his or her reason. You have violated that right, and you can be fined for it. The owner of the property can do anything he wants—within the law—with his property, including allowing it to remain an undisturbed, cool no-picnic spot. It is his, and his rights are specific. Of course, he does not have the right to come onto *your* property any more than you have the right to go onto his.

Private Property Is Private

One property owner owned many hundreds of acres far from town. On the land was a section of hills, gullies, and streams perfect for dune buggies. So, unknown to the owner, a dune buggy club began having their rallies on the property. After all, there wasn't even a PRIVATE sign there. A racecourse was laid out to include the hills and gullies, and on every weekend the club would enjoy the course. It even began to award prizes to the winners in timed runs over the course.

The members of the club didn't think they were hurting anything, though they knew they were on somebody else's property.

This went on for some time, long enough for the ruts from the dune buggies to become almost permanent. In fact, a heavy rainstorm caused a runoff that turned the former wheel tracks into rushing streams. The streams collected and roared down a gully caused by the buggies.

A mile or so "downstream" was a pump house that had been installed by the owner of the land for future irrigation. The runoff rainwater slammed into the pumphouse, ripped it up, and carried it away. The equipment inside—machinery that would never have been touched by the generally honest members of the dune buggy club—was severely damaged.

The land owner learned who had been using his land and deduced what had happened. He visited the site and his suspicions were confirmed. What had happened was obvious. So he sued the club and its members for the full amount of the damage to his equipment. They hadn't damaged his pumphouse and machinery with their dune buggies, they hadn't even been near the pumphouse, but what they had done had ultimately caused the damage.

Since the club treasury didn't contain enough money to pay for the damages, the owner collected the remainder from the members.

Beware of trespassing on private property, whether a sign prohibiting it has been posted or not.

A Sale Can Be a Contract

Thirteen-year-old Janet bought a skirt on sale from a local discount store. Upon wearing it that evening, she found it to be defective. A seam in the skirt had been poorly stitched and was pulling loose. Janet returned the skirt to the store.

But the salesperson refused to listen to Janet. There were adult customers at the counter, and the saleswoman didn't have time for a minor. The sale was final, she said. Everybody knows, she pointed out huffily, that when you buy something on sale, you take your chances.

The salesperson was wrong.

Generally speaking, all purchases are guaranteed at least as to expected performance. If you buy something that breaks down within any guarantee period, or even beyond that period if the breakdown might not be expected, you can get a repair, an exchange, or even a refund.

But what happens if there is no guarantee, or if the breakdown is not covered in the fine print of the guarantee? On all products there is an implied guarantee, one not in writing, for a reasonable period of time after the sale. You must be able to use the item you bought for the purpose that was intended. If it is a hair dryer, it must dry hair. Clothing must be made so that it can be worn as intended.

Janet's skirt did not meet this standard. She pursued the matter with the store manager, pointing out the law of implied guarantee. She showed him the skirt and the defective seam and he, knowing she was right and within the law, immediately offered her an exchange or a refund. He also spoke to the salesclerk about the matter.

More and more in this day of consumer protection, whether you are an adult or a minor, your rights are expanded and explicit. You need never accept a product or a service that does not do what it should reasonably be expected to do. This goes beyond a wheel falling off a car or a meal at a restaurant that makes you ill because it was contaminated. These situations involve serious negligence, and the conclusion is going to be in your favor without much of a battle on your part. But the new protections include much less obvious matters. If a product doesn't work exactly as advertised, you have recourse. Return it to the store and demand satisfaction. People will listen to you because they know the trouble you can cause if they don't.

This right should not be abused any more than any other right, but it can be enjoyed. Don't take any back talk from a snooty salesclerk. You are in the right if you have purchased a defective product. Keep going up the ladder of authority until you find somebody who will listen.

Mail Order Can Be Risky

If Janet had ordered the skirt through the mail she would be on less firm ground. The law says the company must refund her money if the product received is not what was advertised or is defective. The problem is, you have nobody to complain to face to face when dealing through the mail. In a store you can go to the manager and explain your problem. He or she will probably take care of it. If the manager doesn't, you must use other legal means to get the problem solved. This often involves the hiring of an attorney.

Many times, by mail, that is about all you can do. Mail-order houses are far away. They are often faceless. Frequently you will be dealing with a computer. Sometimes it just seems as if you are dealing with a computer. You write a complaint and get back a form letter that may not even respond to your problem.

Most mail-order houses are honest and quickly answer customer complaints. If you return an item, they return your money or make the exchange. But if they ignore you, you are in trouble. The matter is going to take time.

However, if you have received something you feel is not at all within the guidelines of what was advertised, you can also report the company to the Postal Inspection Department of your local post office. They will investigate, and if the seller is guilty of false advertising through the mail, he can be in real legal trouble.

In fact, the threat of being reported to Postal Inspection often brings a human being out of the unresponsive computer front of a mail-order house. Then you have somebody real to deal with, and very often the matter can be handled to everybody's satisfaction. You, as a minor, have just as much right to report a problem to Postal Inspection as any adult.

You might also try reporting the company to your local Better Business Bureau or your district attorney, though it is true that they are more concerned with local cases.

A Product You Didn't Order

Yes, it is true that if you receive a product through the mail unordered and unrequested in any other way (this does not mean a record after you have closed your account at the record club), you may keep it. Be fair about this while you are being firm: Don't accept something you didn't order but that you really want, and then refuse payment. On the other hand, if the sender is dunning you for an unordered, unwanted product, write him that you are going to report him to your local credit bureau or that you are going to send him a bill for storage charges.

Personal Property

Although being a minor has many advantages legally, your age may not protect you from liability if you take, damage, or destroy the personal property of others. Personal property, in this sense, means your personal belongings—your clothing, your car, your books, your furniture—most of the things you own that might be considered to be movable.

Pete borrowed Steve's tape recorder for what he said was only one day. But days passed, then weeks, and finally Pete almost began to consider the recorder as his own and not Steve's. Possession is not a factor here. The recorder is Steve's. Steve had no intention of giving the recorder to Pete. He wanted it back.

If Pete does not return the recorder on demand, Steve may file suit against Pete and will probably collect not only the tape recorder but possibly damages as well.

But what if Pete *found* the recorder? What if he didn't know it belonged to Steve? There is still the responsibility to report the find. In some states, you report it to the police; in others, to the owner of the property where you found the item (a store, a locker room, etc.).

In almost every case, you get the item you've found back after a period of time if the owner does not come forward to claim it. The found item can be equipment, such as a tape recorder, or it can be money. Sometimes it is a lot of money.

One teenager found over $10,000 in a bag next to a trash can. She took it to the police. The police counted the money, then put it away in a safe. The find was made public by newspapers and through classified ads in local publications, as is required in some states by law. The exact amount of money was not disclosed for obvious reasons.

When nobody claimed the money, it was eventually returned to the teenager who found it, and she had a nice nest egg for college.

A Word About Dope

It is doubtful that laws will ever allow teenagers to use a drug such as marijuana, even though recent legislation seems to be easing restrictions on this substance. Much research needs to be done, but in the case of "grass," it begins to appear that it is no more or less dangerous than a substance such as alcohol. It may sooner or later be a controlled substance in the same class as alcohol. But since minors are not allowed the free use of alcohol, they probably will not be permitted the free use of marijuana.

Meanwhile, marijuana is still an illegal substance. The use of the drug can result in penalties that include fines, jail sentences, and suspension or expulsion from school.

To get into more than marijuana does not seem very smart, either. There are certainly many other drugs available to do many other things to your body, or to cause you to think or feel in many other ways. All are illegal and can bring real trouble down upon your shoulders. On top of the legal problems involved, many drugs are addictive and can seriously harm a person's health and cause other problems. One of the most insidious things that drugs can do is use up *time* (and time is what *life* is composed of), with little or no benefit to show for it.

Remember, you do not have to sell one of these substances to break the law. Mere possession is often enough, and that includes possession of not only the drug or narcotic itself, but any injecting or smoking apparatus as well. Visiting a place where narcotics are being used is a crime in many states. You can be arrested for being present at a glue-sniffing or marijuana-smoking party even if you are not partaking.

Here's the bottom line. Federal and state laws make illegal the preparation, transportation, sale, possession and use of certain drugs and narcotics. Harsh penalties can result from violations of these laws. It is especially serious to offer any such controlled substance to a minor, even if the offer is made by another minor.

Your Job Rights

There was a time when sweat shops employed children and young people because they would work cheaply. Bosses worked them long hours and under very poor conditions. Those days are gone forever. Young people have many rights where jobs and employment are the issue.

The federal government regulates employment of minors in places where there is commerce between states. States regulate child labor within their boundaries. Most often these laws and regulations concern the type of employment, hours, and the age of the worker. They also regulate minimum wages.

Young employees can be required to join a union in unionized shops. They pay into Social Security and are in line for Social Security benefits as well as for unemployment compensation and worker's compensation from their state if they are injured on the job. In most states, workers who are minors and who are laid off (or even, in some cases, who *quit* their jobs), can collect unemployment compensation while a state agency tries to locate another job for them. You do not have to be an adult to get these benefits.

If you are not paid for work you have done, you have the same right as any adult to demand your wages. If you are still not paid, you can follow up through local and state agencies (Department of Human Resources, Labor Board, etc.) in your own state. These agencies are there to help in matters such as this, and they will follow up and see that you get what you have coming.

One young man was delivering a pizza for his boss, who remained at the store to make more pizzas. On the way, the young man hit a pedestrian with his automobile. Both the young employee and the pizza store are liable for the injuries to the pedestrian. Along with the many rights you have, you also have certain responsibilities on the job. You can cause great damage to your employer by injuring other persons or property, or being negligent in caring for your employer's property.

Freedom of Speech

The school is holding an assembly. The auditorium is jammed with students from all grades. The coach is speaking from the stage about the big upcoming games. Suddenly some clown near the rear shouts *"Fire!"*

Immediately everybody heads for the doors. Meanwhile, a teacher, hearing the shout, triggers a fire alarm to alert the rest of the school and to notify the fire department. In the auditorium, fear is turning to panic as the doors begin to jam. Before order can be restored, fire trucks are surrounding the school and inside there are several serious injuries.

There was no fire. It was all a big joke.

Funny? NO.

Is someone legally liable? Probably. The student who thought the whole thing would be funny is in serious trouble if he can be identified. Lawsuits are sure to result, and he is the one responsible. As he should be. Yes, we live in a free country and enjoy more freedom of speech than any other country in the world. But that freedom doesn't extend to shouting "Fire!" in a crowded room unless there really is a fire.

6

A Matter of Torts

Consider these two cases.

You will recall Arthur, from Chapter 1, who was horse-playing with an umbrella. He was jabbing at some friends. Accidentally, the point of the umbrella struck Thomas in the temple, killing him. Thomas had been objecting, but Arthur loved to swordplay with his umbrella and wouldn't quit. Both boys are minors.

Morris was a fifteen-year-old bicycle rider of some skill and was perhaps more daring than wise. Knowing better, he swung his bicycle up on the sidewalk to avoid a line of traffic and hit an adult pedestrian. The pedestrian was injured and the police were called.

What are the legal rights of Arthur, of the survivors of Thomas, of Morris, and of the pedestrian who was hit by Morris's bicycle?

On the surface, you might imagine that these tort cases are clear cut. A *tort* is a private wrong (other than a breach of contract) that occurs when one person fails to perform a duty toward another person and this failure injures the person or property of the other person. The wrong is compensable in damages such as money, but it must be a breach of some legally recognized duty. This duty can be as simple as being careful not to cause harm to others, or it can be more complex. It can consist of an act or a failure to act when one should act. Some torts can also be crimes.

A tort can be committed by negligence (injuring somebody with a gun you thought was unloaded), intentional misconduct (purposely punching somebody in an argument), absolute liability (your pet lion gets loose and bites somebody), or strict liability (a manufacturer's defective product injures somebody).

The result of a tort can be unpleasant. Even the names, in legal terms, seem unpleasant. Arthur, who committed a tort, is known as a *tortfeasor.* If that isn't bad enough, Arthur's act in punching at Thomas is called *tortious conduct.*

But what about the duties mentioned? It was Arthur's duty *not* to jab at Thomas, since obviously Thomas didn't want to be jabbed at. Furthermore, Thomas could be hurt by Arthur's jabbing.

It was Morris's duty not to swing up on the sidewalk, endangering pedestrians.

The law imposes these duties on all of us and gives the injured party the right to recover damages from the tortfeasor.

Who Cares?

What is very serious for minors is that this is one area of the law that, with very few exceptions, applies to them. Minors are almost without exception liable for their own torts.

So Arthur has committed a tort, and he is liable even though he is a minor. A minor may be found negligent when he or she fails to exercise as much care as "it is reasonable to expect of children of like age, intelligence, and experience," according to the lawbooks. Law journals refer to you as "children" until you reach majority, even if you are seventeen and one half.

So if others of Arthur's age, intelligence, and experience would not have jabbed at Thomas, and they probably would not, then Arthur must be held responsible for the death of Thomas (unless, as in the state of Michigan, he is under the age of seven). In some states, courts hold that children under the age of seven are incapable of negligence. Other states reject this specific a statement, but feel that a very young infant is not capable of negligent conduct or of intentional wrongdoing.

But Arthur is fourteen and certainly capable of negligent conduct.

Minors are most likely to be sued for intentional or negligent torts, not for absolute or strict liability. It is possible, in fact more than possible, that Thomas's parents can get a very large judgment against Arthur.

So what, you say? Arthur probably has no money. Such a judgment can be collected out of assets Arthur owns today, which might be nothing, or out of assets acquired later. These debts don't just go away over a period of time. They can haunt you for a very long time if you cannot or do not pay them on the spot.

What's worse for Arthur, many judgments for tort liabilities cannot be wiped out by filing for bankruptcy.

On the other hand, it is not likely that Arthur's parents can be held liable for Arthur's problem—not unless his umbrella, which was given to him by his parents, can be shown to be a dangerous instrument.

The same is true with Morris and his bicycle. He probably will be held responsible and liable for the accident to the pedestrian. And though his parents give him his bicycle, it is unlikely that the umbrella will be shown to be a dangerous instrument.

But take the case of Billy, who was given a rifle by his parents as a Christmas gift. Billy's father, a former marine and crack rifleman who was proud of his skill with guns, wanted to raise his son to be responsible. He wanted Billy to know how to handle and care for weapons. So he was training him and, as a reward, Bill received a rifle of his own.

He took it into the woods and was practicing when he heard a noise in a nearby thicket. Without stopping to ascertain the source of the noise, he fired the rifle. The bullet went straight into the brain of a prize stud horse that belonged to a neighboring farmer, killing it.

Billy's parents could be in serious trouble. Many parents, in fact, buy liability insurance, often as a part of their homeowner's insurance, for just such tort liabilities of their minor children.

Some states require a parent to be liable or to provide insurance before their minor children can obtain a driver's license. Also, parents can be held responsible in some states for willful vandalism caused by their minor children (usually up to a specified limit). Certainly if a parent directs a child to commit a tort, or even fails to discourage an action that could result in a tort (dropping rocks from a freeway or turnpike bridge, etc.), he or she can be held liable. Or, as in the case of Billy, if a parent gives a minor child a dangerous instrument, he or she can be held responsible.

Why Focus on Torts?

The laws concerning torts prevent others from interfering in our lives. Other people may not cause our person, our reputation, or our property to be harmed. If someone does cause harm to our person, property, or reputation, the law says we may receive money damages, compensation for the injuries. And under certain circumstances, the law will also punish the tortfeasor.

If somebody hits you over the head and steals your bicycle, that person has committed both a tort and a crime against you. That person can be prosecuted for the crime, and you can recover damages for the tort.

Some torts are *not* crimes. Suppose you are backing your car out of your driveway and bump into your neighbor's car across the street. You have committed a tort, and he can recover damages from you or, more likely, from your insurance company. The whole thing was an accident, not a crime.

But suppose you are angry with your neighbor. You jump into your car, slam it into reverse, and roar out of your driveway. You'll show him! You slam backward into his car on purpose, to settle a score. The damage is the same, but now the tort is also a crime. He can collect damages from you, and you can also be arrested.

Your neighbor can sue you for the damage to his car. You will probably have to pay to have the car repaired, since you caused the damage. And in the latter case, you may also have to face the police.

Any injured party has the right to sue for damages for any injury he has suffered as a result of something another party did. If a person is physically injured, he can collect money for repairs to his body as well as money to compensate for the pain and suffering he has endured. If there is a loss of income, that will be taken into account. So will other expenses caused by the tortfeasor's act.

If a person's emotions are injured by somebody, the injured party can collect for mental and emotional suffering. If a person's reputation is damaged, he or she can sue for and possibly collect an amount of money to compensate for their harm. All of this is done to help the person be restored as nearly as possible to the position he or she was in before the injury or damage occurred.

A court may also award *punitive* damages in a tort action. If the tortfeasor's act is found to be deliberate or intentional, the injured party might recover extra damages over and above the actual costs of the damage or injury. These punitive damages are a way for the court to punish the tortfeasor and help the injured party at the same time.

Recently a famous actress sued a tabloid magazine because of some things it said about her. She won the case and was awarded a large amount of money for the damage to her reputation. Then she was awarded another large sum of money as punitive damages, in addition to the amount she received for the actual damage to her reputation. This way the jury could not only punish the magazine for what it did, but discourage the magazine from doing the same thing again.

Unintentional Torts or I Didn't Really Mean To Do It

There was a famous New York City tort case involving a subway conductor who, in an effort to help a passenger board a train, gave the man a shove through the door. You must know the New York subway system to understand how this could really help a person. The trouble was, the passenger was carrying a box of fireworks wrapped in paper. When he was shoved, he dropped the package and it exploded.

The explosion caused some equipment to fall off a shelf onto a woman standing some distance away. She was injured. How do you suppose this matter was handled?

The court found that the conductor could not reasonably have foreseen that his helpful action could have injured the woman. The subway was not held responsible for her injury. Still, we do owe a duty of reasonable care to everybody around us. We owe this duty to anybody we could reasonably expect to be harmed by our actions and, in some states, even to those persons to whom the harm is not foreseeable.

Negligence is a legal term for carelessness. You have a right to be left alone and not be harmed by the actions of others around you, and you also have the responsibility to be careful not to harm others by your actions. If you do not show this "due care," you can be found to be negligent in a court action—and remember, minors are held liable for their own torts in most instances.

Suppose you are a seventeen-year-old boy on the way to your girl friend's house in your family's car. As you near the house, you glance into the rearview mirror and realize your hair is badly mussed. So you pull out a comb and straighten it. But at that moment you slam into another car.

The situation worsens. The other car bursts into flames and the driver appears to be trapped inside. You are stunned by the impact of the two cars but you hurry to get out and help.

Meanwhile, a passing pedestrian rushes to the other car, fights the door open, reaches in and unhooks the driver's seat belts, and pulls the injured man from the flames. He is a hero. He is also burned on the hands and face and needs prompt medical attention.

You are going to be held responsible for all damages, including the medical expenses of the passerby, even though neither you nor anybody else asked him to interfere and become injured. You have been negligent by attempting to comb your hair without first stopping and parking the car.

There is little doubt that you are responsible for the damages to the first car and driver. And most courts will hold that the pedestrian can recover from you because his actions as a rescuer could reasonably be foreseen. Further, the pedestrian's injuries in the attempt might reasonably be foreseen.

You did not intentionally commit a crime. In fact, you would give almost anything to *undo* what you did. But you are liable for negligence, an unintentional tort.

Don't Forget Contributory Negligence

You also have a duty to protect *yourself* as much as possible. You must avoid actions that carry an unreasonable threat of harm to yourself. If you do not, you can be committing contributory negligence.

Chester was driving home alone one night, speeding, when without warning he came upon a car stalled in the fast lane of the highway. The car was unattended and unlighted. Chester, who had received his driver's license only three weeks before on his sixteenth birthday, hit the brakes as quickly as he could, but still his car slid into the stalled car. Both cars were seriously damaged.

It would seem that Chester would have a clear case against the person who abandoned the car, especially since the driver of the other car had left it to walk home to get some tools to make repairs. No hazard lights had been left blinking, no parking lights, no flares—nothing to warn other drivers.

Although the driver who left his car was negligent, so was Chester. *Contributory negligence* was the court's ruling. Chester should have been driving within the speed limit and in such a manner as to be able to anticipate any problems in the lane ahead. Each driver in this case finally fixed his own car.

In some states (you can look up the rule for your state), contributory negligence may completely bar recovery of damages. In other states, it bars recovery only if it is found to be more than half the cause of the accident. In still others, such as California, the damages are only reduced by the percentage of the fault attributed to the plaintiff. This is called *comparative negligence.*

Finally, There Is Gross Negligence

If negligence is carelessness, then *gross* negligence is outrageous, reckless carelessness. It is still carelessness, and not necessarily a crime, but it is carelessness that might be considered extremely foolish and stupid by most people. Legally, gross negligence is failure to use even slight care.

In some states there is a "guest law" which says that a guest in a car cannot recover for damages from a driver involved in an accident. This law applies to nonpaying passengers or, it is assumed, friends or guests of the driver. If the driver is merely negligent, the passenger may not recover damages in these states. But the passenger can recover damages if the driver can be shown to have been grossly negligent.

Howard is driving John home from school, but carelessly allows his car to drift off the road and hit a tree. John is injured. In a state with the guest law on the books, John would have to prove that Howard was driving in a grossly negligent manner in order to be awarded damages for his injuries. Perhaps Howard was showing off by steering the car from the back seat, or seeing how far he could go with his eyes closed before fear of a collision forced him to open them, or performing some other outrageous, reckless act. In any of these cases, John could probably collect in spite of the guest law.

In states without the guest law, of course, John would have a solid case against Howard merely because Howard carelessly ran off the road.

Check into the laws in your state on this matter so that you know what to do and where you stand if you have a passenger in your car or if you are a passenger in someone else's car. You can call your Department of Motor Vehicles or ask at the library for books on the laws in your state.

7

**Would You
Believe,
More Torts?**

J ack took Jenny and Marilyn to a hockey game at the Forum
in Los Angeles. They had talked about going many times,
and finally the opportunity arrived. Jack was an avid fan of
the Los Angeles Kings, but neither Jenny nor Marilyn had
ever seen a game. Still, Jack had told them of the drama of the
pitched battles on the ice, the lightning fast slap shots that occasionally went up to even the second level of the grandstands,
and the generally exciting atmosphere.

What Jenny and Marilyn did not know was that because of
court findings on *assumption of risk*, they could do nothing
when Marilyn was struck in the face by a puck. Marilyn knew
of the danger, and she "assumed the risk." Of course the people
in the arena gave her first aid and she was not seriously injured.
But her cut did require stitches, and she was in real discomfort
for several days after the game.

Assumption of Risk

A spectator who sits in the front row at a baseball game, then gets hit by a foul tip, generally cannot sue the batter. This is assuming, of course, that the batter did not intend to hit the fan with the ball. Courts have ruled this way in several cases. You know when you take the seat that you could be injured even if it does not say so on the ticket. Not that you cannot sue anyway, of course. Anybody can sue anybody for anything at any time. But whether or not the suit has a chance of winning is something a lawyer can judge beforehand. The lawyer might advise you to forget the whole thing.

If you attend an auto race and sneak over the fence to be nearer the cars, then a car hits you, you have assumed the risk yourself by sneaking over the fence. On the other hand—unlike at a hockey game or a baseball game—if you remain in the stands at an auto race, and a car crashes and bounces into the stands, injuring you, you would have a strong tort case against the track who permitted you to sit there.

You are not assuming the risk of being injured by a car when you remain where the management tells you to remain and where it cannot reasonably be expected that a race car will be.

The Street Angels are having their monthly moonlight drag race up in the hills above town on some deserted streets. They've been doing it for years though it is quite illegal. Occasionally the police will come, and everybody will scatter and head for home.

On this night you have been honored by an invitation to ride in the car of the champion driver during the final race of the evening. With a feeling of excitement and appreciation, you strap in and the race roars off. But this time the driver loses control and the car crashes. You are injured. What are your rights?

Under the laws of assumption of risk you probably have very few rights. You knew when you got into the car that it could crash. It is probably going to be your tough luck when the hospital bill arrives.

Intentional Torts

Remember the opening to Chapter 1 of this book? You were walking home with your girl friend, and a gang of toughs committed assault and then battery on you before you handled them. You beat the leader senseless, and the others ran away. You were in serious trouble for having committed battery.

The same would be true if you were a young woman walking home with your boy friend and you tried to hit back at someone who had assaulted you. Your gender doesn't matter in torts. The fact is that assault was committed on you and your friend. An assault occurs when one person threatens to punch another or do some other imminent bodily harm. As long as the second person is fearful that the threat may be immediately carried out, assault has been committed (even if ultimately the threat is *not* carried out). Assault is illegal.

Assault is committed if somebody points a gun at you and instills in you the fear that he or she is going to shoot it. If you know the gun is empty, no assault is committed, of course, since you are not afraid that you will be shot.

Generally you can receive money damages if you are assaulted, even if you are not actually harmed. If you are harmed, the damages can go up substantially. Suppose you are assaulted and although the person theatening the assault never touches you, you suffer a heart attack. A jury might award you a great deal of money.

How may you defend yourself from an assault? You must act very carefully, for you could be committing battery and be held responsible. Battery, remember, means the hitting or touching of a person without that person's consent. Just touching? That's right.

Barry sneaked up behind Melody in school one day and grabbed her arm. Then he pulled her to him, kissed her on the cheek, patted her affectionately, and released her. Melody was angry and pointed out to Barry that he could be arrested for battery.

"But I didn't *hurt* you!" Barry insisted.

"That doesn't matter," Melody fired back, "you *touched* me."

The truth is, physical harm does not have to result before the matter can be a case of battery. Touching without consent is enough.

The act of battery must be intentional. You can hurt somebody accidentally and not be involved in a battery. Suppose you are climbing a rope in the school gym, slip, and fall to the mat. On the mat is another student doing some warm-ups. You land on him and injure him. This is not battery because it was not intentional.

Nor does all this legal talk mean that you cannot engage in some wrestling or other roughhousing with friends if it is usual for you and your friends to do so. Although the play is intentional (though not reckless or in disregard of somebody else's health), it is not battery. Even if somebody is hurt because of it.

But there are limits. The star quarterback on the football team has let go a long pass. He and most of the other players from both teams are watching the flight of the football and the receiver who is trying to catch it. But with all eyes, or most eyes, on the ball, two big linemen rumble in and hit the quarterback from both sides. Then, before he can get up, one of them punches him in the face, breaking his nose. What's a little roughness penalty if they can get rid of the quarterback, right?

But they have gone beyond the limits of a game where body contact is the norm. The quarterback was able to sue them and collect substantial damages for this intentional tort, even though in a game of football there are frequent injuries, and physical roughness is standard.

Freedom From Confinement

Jack wouldn't allow his girl friend, Marcia, out of his car at the drive-in theater one night. She was angry with Jack for something he had said, and she wanted to walk home. But Jack locked the doors of the car and wouldn't permit her to open them. Soon she was in a panic, begging to be released to go home.

Freedom from confinement is guaranteed by law, and Jack was very wrong for confining Marcia. Legally, the violation is called *false imprisonment,* though four specific elements are required before an act will be found to be false imprisonment. Whoever is confining you in any way, by locking a door or blocking a driveway or even pinning your arms to your sides, must be *intending* to confine you. You must be *aware* that you are being confined and you must *not agree* to be confined. There must be no *reasonable means of escape.* If these four conditions are present, you are being falsely imprisoned, and this is an intentional tort.

Marcia's imprisonment in Jack's car met all four of these conditions, and she could have pursued the matter legally by filing suit against Jack. In this case, though, the two made up when Marcia realized that Jack really cared for her and only wanted to talk to her before she went home.

Assault, Battery, and False Imprisonment

All three of these intentional torts can be present in one situation. Patty, Mindy, Karen, and Sue are having a slumber party at Betty's house, and antagonism breaks out between Karen and Betty. So Betty threatens to scratch Karen's eyes out and pull her hair, frightening her badly (assault). Then Betty shoves Karen into a closet (battery) and locks the door, refusing to free her in spite of her pleas (false imprisonment). Karen has a real case against Betty.

There are certain other intentional torts in law: infliction of emotional distress; conversion (in a civil action, conversion is very much like theft in a criminal action); trespass to chattels (tampering with the personal property of others); and trespass to land.

Consent

The football quarterback certainly gave his consent to be tackled in a football game, so he cannot normally sue for battery if he is tackled especially hard. That's part of the game. He must expect to get hit hard, as hard as the other team can manage. If he doesn't want this to happen, he shouldn't play the game.

As long as the tackles are fair, and at least somewhere within the guidelines of the game, everybody is safe from suit. Of course if a player bent on revenge steps completely outside the rules, the injured player can sue and probably collect.

A girl consents to a pillow fight with a boy, and this removes her chance of charging him with battery. Two boys engage in a boxing match at school, and each tries to hit the other with his fist as hard as he can. Yet since both boys consented, there is no battery. In a school play, one actor threatens another with great bodily harm, but there is no assault.

You must give your consent for an operation, since the doctor is going to cut into your body. Without that consent, the operation would be considered battery. But what if the doctor cuts into the wrong place? You have consented to the removal of your tonsils, and he removes your appendix instead. Then you have a battery and a medical malpractice case.

Of course you must understand what you are consenting to. Scott wants to join a certain fraternity at school. He knows about and agrees to having his hair cut as part of the hazing. He has been told that the members will cut his sideburns off as a sign that he is pledging their group. But then, in a moment of great good humor, they tie him up and shave his entire head. This is battery, since Scott didn't agree to have his head shaved. The fraternity went too far in shaving his head.

Scott's girl friend, in the meantime, has consented to have sexual intercourse with him. She is sixteen. Later the two break up. Scott is secure in the knowledge that since she has given her consent, and since he has done no more than what she consented to, he is in the clear legally. Right?

Wrong. Scott could be in trouble. There are areas in the laws concerning minors in which a minor cannot give consent. Scott's girl friend can sue him for battery, and Scott could also be prosecuted for statutory rape (sexual intercourse with a female under the age of eighteen).

What About Self-defense?

As you strolled away from the gang of toughs, basking in the adoring gaze of your girl friend—or of your boy friend if the situation were reversed—you felt certain you had only defended yourself and your friend from the gang. You know the law gives everybody the right to defend himself. Our country was built on such a right. In the Old West, if someone went for his gun, you had the right to shoot him down.

But this isn't the Old West. According to law, you may use *reasonable force* to defend youself in an emergency. If you can duck the punch from the other guy and try to get away, as humiliating as that might have been in the Old West, you should do it.

If a larger boy is picking on a smaller one, shoving him and taunting him, the smaller boy should attempt to reason with him or avoid a fight. If the smaller boy cannot walk away, he can use only enough force to prevent the large boy from hurting him. If the other boy is pushing, he can push back. But he cannot strike the larger boy with a crippling blow (even if he had the strength to do so) and he cannot, once the danger has passed, continue to hit the larger boy for revenge or for the adoration of friends who might be watching.

If he does, he will be committing a battery, as you did by chopping down the leader of the gang and then continuing to pummel him afterward. He and his parents will probably drag you into court on a battery charge and you may be liable for any injuries he suffered. Certainly a jury will listen to your side, but the law is clear in this area, and that's what the judge will say when he or she instructs the jury. You have used more than reasonable force to defend yourself, and you will probably lose the case.

If you can safely retreat from a deadly force, you must do so. If there is a way to retreat, then you are not privileged to kill in self-defense. Of course, if there is no way to retreat, if your back is against the wall and you are in deadly danger of losing your life, you may defend yourself with whatever means you have, including deadly force.

If you see a larger boy picking on a smaller boy and feel like intervening, you may intervene without risking a charge of battery. You may restrain the larger boy (but not, of course, hit him or injure him) by grabbing him. Normally this would be battery, but in this case it is not.

What if you find a burglar in your house at night? You can hit him first, though normally you should ask a person to leave your property before you attack him. In the case of a burglar, you would not be liable for a charge of battery, because you might well be afraid to talk to him—or to call the police, for that matter. He might hear you calling them and attempt to harm you. So if you are faced with this situation, hit him, *then* call the police (if you feel safe in dealing with the situation at all).

Is a Policeman Liable for Intentional Torts?

Suppose you grabbed a person off the street, clapped handcuffs on him, and threw him in jail. It would be assault and battery and false imprisonment at the very least! But this would not be the case if you are a policeman acting in the line of duty.

Nothing in the law is quite that simple, of course. A policeman needs a warrant to arrest somebody. This is a document issued by a court before an arrest is made. It spells out the officer's right to make the arrest.

Officer Smith was passing by the Second National Bank

when he heard gunshots from inside. Quickly he parked his patrol car and stationed himself by the door. As two bank robbers backed out the door shooting, Officer Smith rushed to a nearby courtroom to get a warrant for their arrest. Then he hurried back to find the bank robbers waiting for him. Then he arrested them.

Unlikely? Of course. Police officers must use judgment in their powers of arrest. If they see a crime being committed, they need not have a warrant. They can make the arrest and take the criminals to jail. But they must arrest the right person. In a recent case, an officer arrested a young man and took him to jail. The man protested that he was innocent, but the officer had a warrant with the man's name and address on it and the description seemed to fit the young man. So the policeman didn't listen to the man.

Later it was found that the man was innocent. Another man, the real criminal, had the same name and a similar address and looked very much like the first man. Later still, the first man received a large settlement from the city because he had been falsely imprisoned.

It is best, if you are involved with a policeman, to do as he says. Policemen understand the danger they are often in, if not with you, then with a real criminal. And they don't know you that well, if at all. So if you are stopped by the police, cooperate and don't make any false moves. Don't reach for identification in your purse or pocket until you are asked to do so. Don't offer arguments or resistance. Your chance to defend yourself will come when you have a lawyer or your parents are present. Don't antagonize a policeman.

Recently a policeman shot and killed a five-year-old child who was holding a toy gun. In a darkened room, the child appeared to the policeman to be a small adult holding a gun. So the policeman shot and the bullet struck the child. The policeman had made a mistake. After a hearing, he was returned to duty. Try not to put yourself in a situation where such a mistake can occur.

Defamation—Slander and Libel

Suzy, a sixteen-year-old student in the tenth grade, simply didn't get along with Mr. Simkins, her science teacher. She didn't like Mr. Simkins personally, and she didn't think he was a very good teacher either. Whether or not Mr. Simkins liked or even thought much about her, Suzy didn't know. But he always gave her failing or near failing grades.

For Suzy, this was hard to take. Not that she was much of a student, but she couldn't accept such grades from a teacher like Mr. Simkins. She decided that she'd get back at him.

So Suzy started telling other students that Mr. Simkins had made a pass at her after class. He had grabbed her and attempted to unbutton her sweater. He had attempted to kiss her, all the time telling her he wanted to make love to her. She was terribly frightened, insisted Suzy. She didn't know what to do. She finally ran away and only later decided to tell the "truth" about what had happened. Of course, the story could have been true. Such things have been known to happen in schools.

Mr. Simkins was called to the school office and appeared so guilty in his nervousness and apprehension that he was suspended and then arrested. He was placed on bail until a hearing could be convened. At the hearing it was determined that he wasn't guilty at all, and that Suzy, who broke down and cried on the stand, was lying. Meanwhile the newspapers had printed story after story about Mr. Simkins, his wife, his children, Suzy, and everybody else connected with the case.

Suzy had injured Mr. Simkins' reputation, and the law attempts to protect us from this type of injury. People base their opinions about you on your reputation. A good reputation is very valuable.

Suzy had defamed Mr. Simkins by first *slandering* him, or saying something derogatory about him. Then she had *libeled* him by writing the lies about him in a note to her friends.

Remember, minors are responsible for their own torts. Mr. Simkins sued Suzy, and in this case received an out-of-court settlement from Suzy's parents, who didn't want the matter to go to court. If it had, Mr. Simkins would probably have won and received a judgment for a great deal of money from Suzy. And the judgment would have been good for years to come, even after Suzy had become an adult and was earning money.

Defamation (which includes both slander and libel) is a serious matter. You are protected from people who would go about saying and writing bad things about you, things that could damage your reputation.

In one case, there was a student who simply didn't like to date girls. He never had and probably never would. He was the type of boy who would probably grow up to be a confirmed bachelor. Another student began to spread the word that the first boy was a homosexual and that was the reason he never dated girls. On the sly, he was dating other boys. So said the one spreading the stories.

Soon the friends of the first student began to drift away from him. They shunned him at games and parties. They believed the stories about him and didn't want anything to do with him.

The first student sued the second and won the case. He was awarded substantial (for a high school student) damages which the second student had to work to pay for. In the end, the lie only enhanced the reputation of the first student, while it cost the second student a lot of money and hard work.

But remember one thing. Truth is a defense against any action of defamation. If you say a person is a homosexual, and he is a homosexual, and you said it without any malice, you are not going to be held liable for damages in a defamation suit.

Invasion of Privacy

Truth may be a defense against the tort of defamation, but it is not a defense against the tort of invasion of privacy.

You are the editor and chief writer for your school newspaper. One of the solid citizens in your town is caught red-handed robbing a local bank. He has been a rock in the community and until that time not a word of scandal has touched him. You can write headlines and a lurid story about him and his crime.

But then you learn in your research on the story that another solid citizen in your town was caught, tried, and convicted for bank robbery ten years ago. That is the truth. It is a matter of public record.

You'd better not put *that* in your story too.

The first story is true, it is news, and you'll be safe from the tort of invasion of privacy if you write it. The second story is also true, but it is not news. The man has paid his debt to society and returned to private life. He is now an obscure citizen living a law-abiding life. You might still be telling the truth if you wrote about him, but now you are a definite target for a suit for invasion of privacy. The truth, the fact that he did rob the bank, will not be a defense. You'll probably lose and be ordered to pay damages unless there is a newsworthy reason for mentioning him.

There is one fact about the tort of invasion of privacy that you should know in case you have the urge to go digging into private lives and then telling what you find. The lives of certain people—public figures such as politicians, movie stars, and leading newsmakers—are not considered to be as private as yours or mine. If you tell the truth about them, they will probably ignore it. If you find out that a leading senator has a criminal record in his past, you can probably write about it and not be a target for an invasion of privacy suit as long as what you write is the truth.

If you lie about a person, even a noteworthy person, that person will probably sue you for committing the tort of defamation.

8

Vehicle Law: Bicycles, Motorcycles, and Cars

The young bicyclist was obviously having a very difficult time. Her bike was lurching back and forth as she tried to balance a bag of groceries and navigate at the same time.

The approaching motorist slowed, but in his heart he felt as some other motorists feel, that bike riders are second-class citizens and should stay off the streets and out of the way. He grinned as he watched the young rider wobble back and forth up ahead. But then, just as he was passing, the cyclist lurched to the left and crashed directly into the side of his car. Damage resulted to both vehicles and the rider was slightly injured with a cut on her arm and bruises.

Who was at fault? According to a later judgment, the motorist was at fault and was held liable for all damages. He should have known that bikes have the same rights as cars, and he should have anticipated that the bike might swerve since he had plenty of time to see that the rider was having difficulty. Thus he should have stopped or given wider berth to the bike.

All vehicles have the same basic rights and must obey the same basic rules of the road. But if you are a cyclist, be careful. Many drivers do not recognize your rights. They will take the section of road they want, and if you are in the way, you will have to move over.

Many communities have ordinances that require every bicycle to be licensed. The bike must be registered with the local police, often after a safety inspection. This assures not only that the bicycle is in good riding condition but that it can be recovered more quickly if it is stolen or lost.

Yes, bicycles must stop for red lights (though some do not) and signal for right or left turns or slowing down. Bicycles must stop at stop signs, too. Your bike must be equipped with a headlight and a tail reflector or light for night riding.

Let's "Borrow" a Bike

Jim knew Andy fairly well since both played on the same high school golf team. Jim came in off the course early while Andy was still out. In the clubroom bike rack sat Andy's brand-new ten-speed. Jim needed to run a quick errand, so, figuring Andy wouldn't mind, he temporarily borrowed the bike. He had no intention of keeping the bike; he just wanted to use it for a short time.

When Andy came in, showered, and got ready to go home, his bike was missing, and he had no idea where it was. By the time Jim finally returned, Andy had not only obtained another ride home, he had notified the police about his "stolen" bike. In fact, the police were at the golf course when Jim returned.

Andy was angry, but he would have allowed the whole matter to blow over once Jim explained. Not the police. Jim had committed a misdemeanor by borrowing the bike without the owner's knowledge or permission, and he was subject to a stiff fine—and a hard lecture from local juvenile authorities. He could even have been held under arrest for a period of time, though in Jim's case this did not happen. It is best not to borrow a bike, or any other personal property for that matter, without permission.

Of course if Jim had stolen Andy's bike, intending not to return it, he would have been committing a more serious crime, and the punishment would have been more severe.

Traffic Laws

Don't count on traffic laws to protect you as a bicyclist or motorcyclist, although in more than one case judges have awarded damage to cyclists when automobiles have made otherwise legal maneuvers, such as left turns in front of them, causing an accident.

The laws work both ways, though. One young cyclist was speeding down a long hill when he saw a truck parked along the curb ahead. In fact, the truck was parked illegally, in a No Parking zone. That didn't matter to the rider. He was certain he could swing out and around the truck and thus not have to slacken the speed he had built up for the climb up the next hill.

He was wrong. Just as it became too late to stop, a car came from the other direction and filled the oncoming lane. The cyclist had nowhere to go. Bracing himself, he rammed into the back end of the truck. He was injured, and his bike was totally wrecked.

Still, he was in the clear, right? The truck, after all, was parked illegally. It shouldn't even have been there in the first place. That should settle the entire matter of fault.

No.

In the litigation between the boy and his parents, and the trucking firm, the court finally ruled that the truck was only partially responsible for the accident. Both the boy and the truck driver had caused the accident.

"A bicycle rider," ruled the court, "has the same duty as any other vehicle operator." The court decided that the boy was out of control in that he could neither stop nor turn to avoid the collision.

Motorcyclists generally realize their vehicle is more similar to a car than a bicycle is and they usually pay more attention to the rules of the road. How often do you see a motorcyclist run a red light or a stop sign compared to how often you see a bicyclist disregard them? Motorcyclists usually have more experience on the roadways and realize the damage a several ton vehicle can do to the unprotected body.

Still, a wise motorcyclist also realizes the attitude many auto drivers have about any two-wheeled vechicle. The wise motorcyclist rides very defensively. One motorcycle rider of long experience said, "I ride as though every other vehicle on the road is trying to run me down. I stay as far away from everybody else as I can, and I always try to allow myself an escape route from every potential collision."

Beware of Buses

The automobile and other motor vehicles have brought into our existence the most complicated maze of laws, rules, regulations, ordinances, requirements, fees, danger—even death—insurance problems, legal hassles, and pleasure ever known to people—especially to young people.

An example? One young man came out of the local drugstore and walked across the sidewalk. At that moment, he saw a friend across the street. He called and waved, attempting to attract the friend's attention, but the friend walked on. Meanwhile, the young man couldn't cross the street even at the corner because of traffic. So he stood next to a streetlight and watched and waited.

At that moment a huge bus came around the corner. It was a tight turn for a bus. A part of the bus extended over the curb and hit the young man. He was knocked into the light pole and injured, though not too seriously. In court, the young man's attorney insisted that the sidewalk was for pedestrians, not buses, and that his client was merely standing on the sidewalk when the bus hit him.

No, argued the bus company's attorney. If you are standing so close to the curb that a bus making an ordinary legal turn hits you, that is negligence on your part. You should watch and be more careful. You should step back if necessary, to avoid being struck.

The court agreed with the young man. It makes no difference where the wheels of the bus are, the bus itself should not be over the curb. A pedestrian should be safe on the sidewalk.

But what if the person on the sidewalk sees the bus coming and notices that it extends over the curb, and yet makes no attempt to avoid the potential accident? That, according to a bus company to whom this actually happened, should make all the difference. After all, if the person sees the bus, it is a matter of merely moving out of the way. So what if a little of the bus extends over the curb?

Wrong again. The court said, "Plaintiff was on the sidewalk where buses do not go, and he had no reason to anticipate that the driver would operate in such a way as to strike people standing at that place. The sidewalk being made exclusively for pedestrians, the bus driver had no right to presume that Plaintiff would step aside and avoid the danger the driver was creating."

Then when are you at fault if you are standing on the sidewalk and get hit by a car or bus? The answer is easy. When you lean out over the curb into the path of whatever is hanging out over the wheels of the vehicle, you are at fault—when you put yourself into the area where the vehicle should be allowed to operate without interference.

Traffic Tickets

Jim, a senior in high school, was in a hurry to get home. He'd promised to take his kid brother to Little League for an important game. It was the first time the kid was going to pitch, and Jim was looking forward to the occasion. So Jim drove quickly down Main Street, cut up Maple, and squealed around the corner of Elm, his street. He wasn't looking behind most of the way.

He should have been, for Officer Krupke was following half a block further back. The trouble with Officer Krupke, according to everybody at school, was that he had it in for kids with cars. Old Krupke hadn't had a car until he joined the force, and it seemed he frowned on anybody under thirty who owned one. He was grinning broadly when he flipped on his "bubble machine" and tapped on the siren.

"Oh, no!" Jim groaned, pulling over to the curb.

"Going to a fire, kid?" Officer Krupke asked.

"Yeah, well, I'm sorry, Officer Krupke," Jim said, "but I'm on the way home to take my kid brother to a game and I guess . . . well . . . I suppose I was going just a little bit fast."

"A little bit," the policeman shot back, "you were going at least twenty miles over the limit!" With that, he pulled out his ticket book and started writing. Jim was shocked. Sure, he might have been going a little over the speed limit, and he shouldn't have been, but he knew he hadn't been going twenty miles per hour over the limit. Officer Krupke asked for Jim's driver's license, completed the ticket, and handed it over for Jim's signature.

"I'm not signing anything," Jim stated. "I'm not guilty and I'm not signing anything that might show up in court—which is where I will see you."

With a sigh, Officer Krupke ripped off Jim's copy of the ticket, handed it to him, and returned to his cruiser.

Was Jim right? Would he be admitting guilt if he signed the ticket?

No, to both questions. Signing a traffic ticket is not an admission of guilt, but only a promise to appear in court, or to post bail, according to the instructions on the ticket. Not signing it will do nothing for you and could hurt you in case the officer wanted to pursue the fact that you are being uncooperative and refusing to promise to appear. The officer probably won't, but he or she could arrest you for refusing to sign the ticket.

Speaking of tickets, here's a hint when you are stopped by the police. Remember, they don't like sudden moves and possibly concealed weapons. Don't get out of your car to go and meet the officer. Remain in the driver's seat with both hands visible on the steering wheel. Don't reach into your pocket for your license until the officer asks for it. Certainly don't reach for anything in the glove compartment until he or she is at the window giving you specific instructions on what to do. The officer could mistake your move for an attempt to reach for a gun, and by the time you had a chance to explain, it could be too late.

It generally does little good to argue with a police officer, but by the same token you don't have to be any more than polite. After all, getting at ticket isn't a happy occasion so why should you have to smile and keep saying "sir" or "ma'am" and "I'm sorry?" The officer isn't judge and jury. You are still innocent. You have, in his or her opinion, broken a law. Either you will decide the police officer is right (or that it simply isn't worth fighting) and pay the bail or fine to avoid going to court, or you will take advantage of your opportunity to "fight" the ticket by appearing in court.

If you go to court, you will be given a chance to plead either not guilty, guilty, or, in some states, *nolo contendere* (you are in effect pleading guilty but not really admitting it in court, so that a guilty plea cannot later be used against you in a civil suit). With the latter two pleas, the judge will fine you or do whatever he or she decides in the case, and the matter will be over—unless, of course, you must serve some time in a juvenile facility.

If you decide to plead not guilty, show up in court dressed neatly and with all the facts you need handy. You will be given a chance to choose between a jury trial and a hearing before a judge, and a date for the trial will be set.

Suppose you just ignore the whole thing? Sure, you got a ticket, but you lost it and besides, it wasn't very important. In this case, a warrant could be issued, and you could be arrested. This could mean loss of your driver's license. Remember how hard you worked for it?

If you get a ticket, take care of it the legal way.

Unlawful Use of a Vehicle

Jerry didn't mean to steal Don's beautiful new car. But there it was, keys in the ignition and waiting in the school parking lot. So Jerry convinced his girl friend that Don wouldn't mind if they "borrowed" the car for a quick joyride. The trouble was, Don didn't know that Jerry had the car, and so he reported it stolen.

Remember when Jim took Andy's bike from outside the clubhouse at the golf course without permission? Andy was angry, but Jim didn't get into too much trouble. With a car it can be different, very different. In some states the offense is grand larceny, and in other states special laws make intentional joyriding similar to petty larceny, but in every state it is very serious business. Jerry might be fined a couple of hundred dollars if he is caught, or he could spend some time in a juvenile facility.

Over one-half of all the auto thefts in the United States are committed by people under the age of eighteen. So police and courts are wary of minors joyriding in cars. Who is to know whether or not the minor intended to steal the car?

If you are under eighteen and caught joyriding and have no prior offenses with regard to auto theft, you will probably get probation in most states. If you have a prior history of joyriding, look out.

He Said It Was Safe To Pass

You are driving along a two-lane highway behind a huge truck. He is going thirty; you wish to go fifty-five. But he lumbers along, mile after mile, uphill and down, around this curve and that. You ramble along behind him, waiting for a chance to pass. The problem is, it is very difficult to see around him. So you wait . . . and wait . . . and wait.

Then, at last, it appears there will be a longer, straighter stretch of road ahead. As if to confirm it, you see the directionals on the truck ahead begin to blink for a left turn. At the same time, you see the driver waving his arm out the window, telling you it is safe to pass.

So you swing out and only at that moment do you discover two facts. The truck in front of you is following another truck very closely, narrowing down the safe margin for you to pass in, and up ahead there is a rapidly approaching oncoming car. By then you are halfway past the truck. You apply the brakes and try to swing back in behind the second truck, but it is too late. You hit the other car a glancing blow and both of you wind up in the ditch.

So, after you get out of the hospital and look at the lawsuit you are facing from the driver of the other car, you decide to get a lawyer and sue the truck driver who waved you on and the trucking company he represents. After all, the accident wouldn't have happened if he hadn't waved you on.

No, insist the lawyers for the trucking company. Sure, their driver was trying to help. Their driver knew that he was obstructing the road, that he had been blocking you for many miles and that he might help you by waving you around. But he is no policeman. You were under no obligation to follow his signal. It was up to you to pass on your own, to make your own decision.

If you had exercised due caution, said the lawyers for the trucking company, the accident wouldn't have occurred. This case actually happened and in most states the court's decision would be the same. Once the truck driver decided to give directions to the following car, he took on the duty to be careful. He failed in this duty and so the trucking company was held liable for the accident.

Would the same be true if a policeman gave the signal to move? It happened once. A motorist was waiting at a traffic light when a policeman, who was trying to unsnarl a traffic jam, waved him forward. He did it with such a dramatic wave and blow of his whistle that the tense motorist allowed his car to leap forward.

The car hit a pedestrian who happened to be right in front, injuring him seriously. The pedestrian sued the driver, and the driver sued the city, who employed the policeman. The driver insisted that he would not have moved at all except for the frantic blowing of the whistle and the insistent waving of the officer's arm. Thus the city should be held liable for the accident, not the driver of the car.

Not a chance, ruled the court. Nobody forces anybody to run over a pedestrian. The driver should have used more caution no matter how hard the officer was blowing his whistle or waving.

What To Do If You Have an Accident

Did you know that you have a fifty-fifty chance of having an accident during your driving life? It may be a simple fender-bender, or it may be very serious. In either case, there are certain things to do to increase safety and prevent later legal problems.

But first, suppose you hit an unattended car. Leave a note under the windshield wiper blade listing your name, address, telephone number, and car license number. Some drivers also leave their insurance policy number and the name of the company. In this way the damaged driver can go directly to your insurance company (which you have contacted in the meantime, of course).

You may have heard the old joke about the man who backed

into another car, damaging the door. He got out, looking at the damage, then dug out a paper and pencil and began writing a note.

"Everybody standing around watching," he wrote, "thinks I am leaving you my name and address, but I'm not."

Then he put the note under the windshield wiper blade and drove away. That was not nice. Nor was it legal. Anyone who really wrote such a note would be in a lot of trouble if he were caught. In fact, this is one of the first rules of conduct after you have had an accident.

1. Stop at once. Do not drive away. Even if the damage seems very slight to you, stop in a safe place and, at night, place flares or get somebody to direct traffic around the accident.
2. If anybody is hurt, call an ambulance. You will have to move people if they are in a burning car or on the highway, but otherwise don't move injured people.
3. Notify the police.
4. Exchange driver's license information with the other driver. Show your auto registration and ask to see his, then copy down the information.
5. See if you can locate any witnesses to the accident. If you can, write down their names and addresses. This can be very important to you if you will be attempting to recover damages from the other party.
6. Write down where and when the accident occurred and also write down the names and addresses of every passenger in each car involved.
7. As soon as you can, diagram the accident and write down your own observations about how it happened. Make notes of weather conditions, road conditions, and visibility as well as speed limit signs, traffic signals, crosswalks, and other traffic control markers. If you have a camera, take pictures of the cars, the passengers, the skid marks, and other items that might

help later to show how the accident occurred and who was involved.

8. Do not admit liability for the accident to anybody, including the police, unless you are advised to do so by your lawyer. Do not speak to anybody if you are dazed or hurt unless it is to give the required information on driver's license and car registration. Do not sign any statement about the accident until you have had legal advice. If somebody says the accident was your fault, say "That is your opinion," and let it drop.

9. Most states require some type of liability insurance. Without it, you may lose your driver's license. So be prepared to prove you are insured.

10. If you have been injured, even slightly, get an examination by your doctor as soon as possible after the accident. Take photos of your injuries, if possible.

11. Notify your insurance company as soon as possible after the accident. Notify your lawyer if you have been in an accident where you or anybody else was injured, or where you have been charged with a traffic violation as a result of an accident.

9

More Vehicle Law: Insurance, Accidents, and Searches

Consider the plight of John, who parked his car near an exclusive apartment house before visiting a friend. He had no way of knowing that an apartment in the building was at that very moment being ransacked by a burglar. He had parked his car right below the window of that particular apartment.

While John was with his friend, the burglar was discovered. Thinking quickly, he leaped out the window—directly onto the hood of John's car. The hood caved in, the burglar bounced off, and with hardly a backward glance, he streaked away into the night. By the time the police arrived, the crook was long gone.

Amusing, John admitted when he learned what had happened. But not a major problem. The next day he drove to his insurance agent and asked where he should take his car for repair.

"Repair?" asked the agent. "This is not a covered accident."

The insurance policy, explained the agent, does not cover something such as a burglar jumping on top of your car.

"But wait a minute," John protested. "If this isn't 'collison' I don't know what it is. He collided with my car and damaged the hood."

"No way," said the agent. "You're out of luck."

So John retained an attorney and sued the insurance company for the damages to his car, plus the costs of the lawyer. And he won the case.

"Collision means the impact of objects through one of such objects moving against the other," ruled the judge. The burglar was an object in the strictest sense of the insurance policy, and the car was the other object. So what happened fit into the spirit of the policy. The company paid for John's car repairs and for his legal expenses, too.

You can only stretch this so far, though. One young driver wanted to collect on his collision coverage when his car was bombarded with hailstones during a storm.

"We do not speak of falling bodies, such as sleet or hail, as 'colliding' with the earth," decided the court in one state. "In common parlance, the apple falls to the ground; it does not collide with the earth. So with all falling bodies, especially where the fall is purely the result of the laws of nature, such as snow, sleet, hail. We speak of the descent of such bodies as a fall to earth, not a collision with it."

About Insurance

Most states require drivers to have some form of liability insurance or the ability to be financially responsible for any accident.

Scott asked his dad if he could use the family car to go and pick up his friend, Joe, from the airport. "OK," said his dad, "but be careful."

The trouble was, on the way home Joe persuaded Scott to allow him to drive the car. Joe lost control of the car, it careened across the street, and slammed directly into another car. The man driving the other car was killed.

The widow of the man sued Joe, Scott, and Scott's parents for more than $100,000 in damages for herself and her two children. They won a judgment for that amount against Joe's and Scott's parents. The insurance company of Scott's parents paid $10,000, which was the limit of their liability insurance; Scott's parents had no property or money to satisfy the balance of the judgment. That left $90,000 for Joe to pay, and Joe had no money at all. Joe's parents' insurance policy covered Joe only while he was driving his family's car. Meanwhile, the court took Joe's driver's license away.

Was that the end of the story?

Not by any means. Later, Joe got a job in a store, but the widow had his wages garnisheed, and the store, not wanting to bother with legal matters, fired him. Several years later, Joe received some money from the estate of his parents, and it was immediately taken by the widow who had the judgment against him. Because he was careless, Joe will be paying on the judgment for many years. Unless he does very well financially, he will probably never get it paid off, since now the interest on the amount increases faster than he can pay on the principal.

Be Careful of "Emergencies" in a Car

There was the case of the truck driver with a load of dynamite. Going down a long hill, he suddenly realized his brakes were failing. He could slow the truck, but he couldn't stop it. Worse, the brakes were giving out right under his foot. He had to do something, and fast. So he jumped. It was all he could think to do at the time. The truck rolled on, picking up speed as it rushed down the hill.

Now for the question. If the truck hits something and does some damage, who is responsible?

There is an *emergency doctrine* often used by courts to solve such problems as this, and in this case, under that doctrine, the driver was not held liable for the resulting explosion, which injured some onlookers. The court held that the driver was "compelled to act by the instinct of self-preservation." His duty to others was considerably less than his duty to himself.

The emergency doctrine can affect you.

Suppose you are driving down the street minding your own business, paying attention to where you are going and doing a generally good job of getting from one place to another in your car. This is important, as you will see, since later questions in court may try to uncover the fact that you were looking around at sale signs in store windows or at the people walking up and down the street or at some other distraction.

But you are paying attention.

Suddenly and without warning, a child dashes out between two parked cars directly into your path. You are not speeding, but there is no way you can stop in time. You hit the brakes hard and swerve to the left, which is the only way you can go without slamming into parked cars. You miss the child, but only then do you realize that there is an oncoming car in the lane you have just entered and you are facing an immediate head-on collision.

All you can do is swerve back again, and by this time you are effectively out of control. Your car jumps up on the sidewalk, bounces back out over the curb, and slams into a parked car. Considerable damage is done to both you car and the parked car, but the child is safe.

You figure you are in very serious trouble, but later in court you see the emergency doctrine in use. You are found not liable for the accident. There was nothing else you could do under the circumstances.

But this doctrine cannot be stretched indefinitely. It has been designed to ensure that it cannot be taken advantage of. For example, if it can be shown that you were not paying attention to your driving, you can and probably will (and probably should) be found liable.

Keep the emergency doctrine in mind if you have a relevant accident. It could help you.

When Is Red Green?

In one word, *never!*

It will never, never pay to run through a red light. If you don't have an accident, you can get a costly ticket. Everybody knows that. But what if you accidentally run through a red light, catching it when it is changing instead of pure red? Suppose you come up to an intersection and the light is green? Then suddenly, without warning and without a caution light, it turns red. This happened to one young driver. What was worse, there was another car entering the intersection from the other direction. The two cars came together with a loud crash.

Later, in court, the young driver insisted that the city was at fault because the traffic light was defective. The caution light was not functioning and for that reason he had no idea the light was about to turn red. Meanwhile, the other driver was merely going through a green light.

The city admitted it was at fault in the sense that the light was not working correctly, but it also pointed out that it would be impossible for a city to perfectly maintain every mechanical device every minute of every day. The city attorney listed all the things that could go wrong, the devices that must be constantly maintained. Citizens, he argued, should be aware and allow for malfunctions.

In this case the court found for the young driver. Why? Not because the city's light was malfunctioning, but because it had been malfunctioning for more than a week. In that length of time, decided the court, the city should have become aware of the light and had it fixed. Instead, it was allowed to malfunction. So the city had to pay.

Accidents Between Young Drivers

You do have a problem as a minor. Your insurance rates are very high because you have a disproportionate number of accidents for the number of minors driving. You are, as a group (but certainly not as individuals, since most will agree that the superior eyesight and reflexes of young drivers should make them better drivers than adults), not very safe on the road. You should be very proud of your accident-free record if you have one.

There is a reason why most insurance companies give better rates to better students and to students with a safe driving record. Better students have learned to think for themselves, to work hard to get something right, to study something out, to keep from goofing around. What they do in the classroom reflects what they do on the road.

Students with good driving records and no tickets or accidents have shown they know how to drive. Very often an accident between young drivers goes unreported because of the possible rise in insurance rates, or because it is impossible to determine who is at fault and neither driver wants to make a big deal out of the situation. So each driver fixes his own car, and the matter is dropped. Of course you can't do this if someone is injured, or if there is major property damage, but otherwise both parties often just keep the matter between themselves.

Ben ran into Martha's car as the two were leaving the school parking lot. The fault was Ben's and Martha was totally blameless. Still, Ben refused to pay for the damages he had done to Martha's car. He even refused to go to his insurance company since, although the damage was less than $300, he was afraid his rates might go up, or he might be dropped from the "good driver" status.

None of that mattered to Martha, who had to suffer with her bashed fender every day. Martha was a stickler for neatness and though she liked Ben well enough, she finally could tolerate the fender no longer. She went to a lawyer.

The lawyer wrote a letter to Ben's insurance company. The insurance company spoke with Ben. Then the insurance company made a settlement for the full amount of the damage to Martha's car and the lawyer's fees as well. Nor did Ben's insurance rates go up. Not this time, although if it should happen again, the insurance company might raise the rate or even drop their coverage of Ben's car.

Minors are in a difficult position with insurance, since there is such a high percentage of accidents among teenage drivers. This makes insurance companies nervous, and they tend to react when your name comes up more than once or twice.

It's up to you. Laws vary from state to state, but most states require an accident report only if there is a certain amount of damage or if there have been injuries. Possibly it would be best to work things out privately with the other person involved in the accident.

May the Police Search Your Car?

In a word, probably. But not certainly. You see them searching your friends' cars on cruise night in town. Do they have the right? In the strictest legal sense, the police can only search your car:

1. if you give them permission, or
2. if they have a search warrant, or

the trickiest reason—

3. if they have probable cause

If the police stop you for something—speeding, reckless driving, running a light, or some other traffic problem—and you have a funny-looking cigarette dangling from your lips, they will probably search your car. And they will be able to use any evidence they find against you in court, even though you might argue that they had no reason to search your car and that the evidence should be excluded. Anything that is illegal and in "plain view," such as a gun on the seat beside you or a beer can on the floor, will give the police the probable cause necessary for a search.

On the other hand, if you are stopped for a routine traffic violation and the officer simply takes a dislike to you, he has no right to search your car. He may ask you to open your glove compartment or your trunk, and from a strict legal standpoint you can do it or not. It's up to you. But you know what might happen if you don't do it. The officer is going to suspect that you are hiding something, and he may just decide he has probable cause and go ahead and search anyhow. Don't resist. If necessary, fight it out in the courtroom.

In some states, officers can merely impound your car, have it hauled away, and then get a search warrant from a friendly judge. If they find anything in the car that shouldn't be there, they are on solid legal ground. If they don't find anything, they can say they are sorry. They do have a point, you know. Houses are much more carefully protected against illegal search than cars, since you can't move a house, but you can move and hide a car. By the time the police get a search warrant, a car can be long gone. So laws are a bit more flexible when it comes to searching cars.

If the police really want to see what you have in your trunk, they can probably figure out a way to do it. So here's the best advice: Don't carry anything incriminating around in your car.

10

Understand Juvenile Court

Jeff, Martha, and Wally were sitting around Martha's pool smoking marijuana. They were talking about this and that, and finally one of them suggested robbing the local liquor store.

Why? Nobody could remember later. Oh, they recalled talking about Jeff's overdue car payment to his parents and a new dress Martha wanted very much, but there was nothing specific about needing the money that badly. Still, the idea seemed attractive, especially when Martha piped up with the fact that her father kept a handgun in the dresser beside his bed.

"Let's see it," demanded Jeff, so Martha went to get it. Wally, usually one to follow rather than lead, simply listened, nodding his head.

"All right!" exclaimed Jeff when Martha handed him the gun. "Now, how about some stockings for masks?"

Martha hurried for some stockings and soon the three were heading for the local liquor store in Jeff's car. They pulled into the parking lot, eased up in front of the store, and turned off the engine.

From inside, the young clerk noticed them. He was a student attending a nearby college, working to pay his way. He realized the three teenagers were acting strangely, but when he saw them put on the stocking masks, he knew there was trouble ahead. So he alerted the police.

With gun in hand and mask in place, Jeff led the other two into the store. Fortunately, there were no customers inside or the tragedy about to happen could have been even worse. For when Jeff brandished the gun at the young clerk, the clerk reached under the counter for the store's weapon. In that instant, Jeff, who did not even know if his own gun had been loaded, pulled the trigger. Twice.

Crack! . . . *Crack!* . . . The reports slammed through the store.

With a look of complete surprise and then sadness, the young clerk slipped to the floor, dead.

Suddenly alert and aware, Jeff turned to Martha and Wally, a helpless, terrified look on his face. Then the three turned and dashed from the store—into the arms of heavily armed, waiting policemen.

Jeff, Martha, and Wally are about to learn firsthand about the juvenile court system now in operation in the United States—and about the many rights and responsibilities of minors when they are in very serious trouble.

A Bit of History

Juvenile courts are not new. In fact, juvenile justice systems began hundreds of years ago in medieval England. According to English common law, the king was the *pater patriae* (father of his country). As such, he was the caretaker of neglected children or of children who had no parents to care for them. From the king came rulings about children in trouble.

When the United States began a separate system of justice for minors in 1899, the people who fought for it patterned our law after the English system even though it left much to be desired. The idea was that the court would be a benevolent father to children in trouble. These courts felt that an adult judge could handle any matter, and that rehabilitation was much more important than punishment. They also felt, however, that a minor who would cheat or steal or harm others should be removed from contact with the rest of society.

So until as late as 1961, and even later—because of the fact that certain matters had to go to the Supreme Court before they became recognized law—juvenile courts were mere hearings before a judge. The judge would listen to the probation department's description of what the minor had done, he would listen to the minor's side of the matter, then he would decide.

Suppose twelve-year-old Alfred is accused of stealing the hubcaps from Mr. Kinkaid's car. The probation officer might suggest that evidence indicates Alfred has stolen the hubcaps because the police found them in Alfred's garage. The probation department, then, is convinced of Alfred's guilt.

"Did you take the hubcaps from Mr. Kinkaid's car?" the judge might ask Alfred. Alfred might be frightened and confused, or he might be trying to protect a friend. Or he might not understand the seriousness of the matter.

The judge will make a decision based on the probation department's reports and on what Alfred has to say in his own defense.

Modernizing the Law

Wait a minute! Where was "due process" in the way things were being handled? Many lawyers interested in the rights of minors began to argue with this sytem. Some parents and interested bystanders felt the same way. For one thing, minors weren't getting fair notice of what they were accused of doing. Police were merely coming and hauling them away. Nobody was really explaining the charges. A minor wasn't permitted to have a lawyer defend him in a juvenile court proceeding. It was all up to the judge and the probation department, with no legal advocate to guard the rights of the accused.

What was worse, the minor had no right to confront the person accusing him, nor any right to cross-examine that person under oath. No witness was even under oath in the juvenile court proceeding.

Finally, and one of the most serious matters of all, nobody kept notes at a juvenile trial. There was no court reporter to keep a record of what was said and who was accusing whom. Thus there was no way that an appeal could logically be made.

So the juvenile laws began to change, state by state. Then, finally, the U.S. Supreme Court heard three cases regarding juvenile rights that set forth certain rights for juveniles in all the states. These three landmark cases were the *Kent* case (1966), the *Gault* case (1967), and the *Winship* case (1970).

With each of these cases, the rights of minors were explained and expanded. Every minor should know about these cases and understand his or her rights in case of serious trouble.

Kent v. *The United States*

In Washington, D.C., an intruder entered an apartment and raped and robbed the woman who lived there. Fingerprints were found and identified, and the police soon arrested sixteen-year-old Morris Kent.

After sessions of questioning during which police confronted Morris with the fact that they knew he was even then on probation for breaking into several homes and for attempting to snatch a woman's purse, he confessed. He had robbed and raped the woman, he admitted, and furthermore, he had committed other similar crimes.

The trouble was, the police had held Morris for more than a week without a charge.

Still, a preliminary hearing was ordered and Morris's mother hired an attorney for advice. The attorney was afraid Morris would be sent to an adult court for trial, so he tried to reason with the judge. He tried to tell the judge that Morris was mentally ill and should not stand trial as an adult. He had Morris examined by a psychiatrist, who said that Morris was severely ill and needed treatment.

The judge didn't want to listen, nor did he allow the attorney to see the probation report. There wasn't even a juvenile court trial. The judge merely sent the case to an adult court "due to the seriousness of the crimes." And that was that.

The adult court found Morris guilty of housebreaking and robbery, but not guilty of rape by reason of insanity. He was sent to an institution for the criminally insane for treatment. He was also sentenced to from thirty to ninety years for the housebreaking and the robbery.

Immediately the lawyer helped Morris appeal his case, and it went to the U.S. Supreme Court. There the justices found that Morris's rights had been violated because of the judge's decision to send the case to an adult court without giving sound legal reasons.

When the justices handed down their decision, which then became the law in all of the United States, certain new rights for minors were created:

1. There must be a full hearing before a juvenile case can be sent to an adult court.
2. The probation department must make a full and complete investigation of the minor's background.
3. Every minor is entitled to full representation in a juvenile court hearing and his lawyer has a right to see all the records available to the judge. The attorney also has the right to question the accuracy of the records.
4. The court must make a full investigation of the case so that any higher court can review the decision. The juvenile court's report must state the specific reasons for sending the minor to an adult court.

These are protections for you.

The *Gault* Case

When Mrs. Cook picked up her telephone one day in Arizona, she didn't expect to hear the indecent remarks she heard. But she was sure she knew the voice and soon the police arrived at the home of Gerald Gault, a fifteen-year-old already on probation for being with another boy who stole a woman's wallet. Gerald's parents were both at work, so the police took Gerald away. Nobody even told the parents their son had been arrested.

When Mrs. Gault arrived home that night, she was worried. She finally called the police and they told her what had happened. They also said there would be a hearing the very next afternoon.

During questioning at the hearing, Gerald admitted that he had dialed Mrs. Cook's number, but insisted that it was somebody else who had said the obscene things to her. Mrs. Cook wasn't at the hearing. No witnesses were at the hearing, nobody was sworn to tell the truth, and no record was kept of what was said.

Gerald was released temporarily but told to report back for a second hearing. At the second hearing, with Mrs. Cook once again not present, Gerald was ordered to a state industrial school to serve until he was twenty-one years old. That would mean that he would serve a term of six years for the alleged obscene phone call.

The sentence for an adult convicted in a court of law for making an obscene phone call would have been up to two months in county jail, maximum, and a fine of up to $50, maximum.

So Gerald took his case to the U.S. Supreme Court on the basis that he had been denied *due process.*

"He did not have a chance to confront his accuser," said Gerald's lawyer, "and he did not have enough advance notice of the hearing so that he could prepare his defense."

Again the Supreme Court found in favor of the minor. The court found that the due process clause in the Fourteenth

Amendment, which protects adults from hurried actions without representation, also applies to juveniles and juvenile court proceedings. Then the court listed more rights held by minors:

1. A juvenile has a right to written notice of the charges against him, and the notice must tell him exactly which law he is accused of breaking. The notice must also allow him ample time to prepare a defense against the charge.
2. A juvenile has the right to counsel, to have an attorney with him through every stage of the proceedings. If his parents cannot afford a lawyer, then the court must appoint and pay for one.
3. A juvenile must be told that he does not have to testify or make any statement in a trial. Any out-of-court confession must be backed up by some additional solid evidence.
4. A juvenile has the right to confront any witnesses against him, and these witnesses can be cross-examined, under oath, by the judge and by the juvenile's attorney. Only competent and relevant evidence should be admitted during the hearing, while hearsay evidence should be ignored.

These are rights every minor needs to be aware of when he or she is in serious trouble.

The *Winship* Case

Twelve-year-old Samuel Winship was arrested soon after it was discovered that a locker in a department store had been rifled. More than $100 was missing. Samuel's case was heard in a family court, and family members insisted that Samuel had been home at the time of the theft. The trouble was, there wasn't enough evidence on either side to really prove or disprove the case against Samuel.

So the judge, in accordance with the way things were done in juvenile matters in 1970, declared Samuel a "delinquent" and sent him to a reformatory for eighteen months. He could do this because juveniles didn't have to be proven guilty "beyond a reasonable doubt." Just a little more evidence on one side of the case than the other was enough to tip the scales of justice in a juvenile matter. The judge felt that although there was evidence indicating Samuel's innocence, there was more indicating his guilt.

No, said the Supreme Court when the matter reached this high tribunal. The justices listened when Samuel's attorney told them, "Samuel has been deprived of his liberty for something that would have been considered a crime if committed by an adult. Therefore, Samuel is entitled to the same standard of proof that an adult would receive."

What the attorney meant was that Samuel had the same right as an adult. The court agreed, and said that from that point on, juveniles, like adults, had to be proven guilty beyond a reasonable doubt.

Not every justice agreed. Justices Warren Berger and Potter Stewart wrote a dissenting opinion on the *Winship* decision which said, in part, "what the juvenile court system needs is not more but less of the trappings of legal procedure and judicial formalism; the juvenile court system requires breathing room and flexibility in order to survive, if it can survive the repeated assaults from this Court."

What About a Juvenile in an Adult Court?

All of this does not mean that you cannot be tried in an adult court as a juvenile. Jeff, Martha, and Wally might end up in an adult court since no matter how you look at it, they committed cold-blooded murder.

There was a case recently in San Diego, California, when a young high school student who said she was bored began to take potshots at people in the schoolyard across the street. She used a rifle that she was well qualified to use and before she was stopped she had killed the principal and the school custodian and wounded eight students and a police officer.

During the several hours she was fortified in her home and shooting, she told a reporter by telephone that she was shooting to "liven up the day. I don't like Mondays."

Although still a minor at seventeen, she was tried in an adult court because she was found to be accountable as an adult. She pleaded guilty to two counts of murder and as a part of a *plea bargain* (where the accused agrees to plead guilty to one or more offenses and the prosecution agrees to drop certain other charges), it was agreed to drop the "special circumstances" that might have resulted in her being sentenced to death, or life in prison. She was sentenced to twenty-five years, and she is still serving that sentence in California.

Most states have courts for minors called *juvenile court*, or *children's court*, or *family court*. Generally speaking, the minimum age for transfer of a juvenile to an adult criminal court for trial ranges from thirteen to sixteen.

A child under the age of seven was always thought to lack criminal capacity. That is, a child that young simply didn't have the mind to conceive of a criminal act. He or she might do something wrong, very wrong, but it was said that someone so young didn't really understand the wrong.

By the same token, a child of fourteen was said to be able to understand his actions, good or bad. Between the ages of seven and fourteen, lawyers argued in each individual case as to whether the child knew or didn't know right from wrong.

In the past few years, most states have upped the age of criminal responsibililty to eighteen, though some states still use sixteen, seventeen, or nineteen.

What Do *You* Want?

The rights discussed in this chapter are yours. Do you really want all of them? Think about it. With them comes a great deal of responsibility. If you choose the right to a trial by jury, then you must accept that your trial might be open to the public. Do you want a newspaper reporter covering your trial and putting your name in the paper along with the act you are alleged to have committed?

Do you want all of these rights when it could mean that if you lose in court you could be sent not to a relatively pleasant home for youngsters, but rather to a state prison with hardened offenders all around?

Think about it.

11

If You Are
Arrested

Jeff, Martha, and Wally are in serious trouble, but they will not, even though all three are equally guilty of the killing of the young store clerk, face execution or even life imprisonment. They are minors and will probably be handled as minors. They could be said to have been under the influence of a controlled substance at the time of the killing and thus not completely responsible for what happened.

Obviously they did not fully plan the crime. It was almost a spur-of-the-moment action. It was, as their lawyer will surely argue, a "lark." Yet, somebody paid dearly for the lark, and so will Jeff, Martha, and Wally pay, but they will not pay for the rest of their lives beyond the guilt they will carry.

For example, a similarly unplanned but tragic crime occurred several years ago in a Western state. Two young high school lovers were coming home from a dance. They were

walking hand in hand and chanced to cross the high school ath-
letic field along the way. Perhaps overcome by the beautiful,
warm night, a lovely moon overhead, their deep feelings for
each other, and the fact that they were alone, they paused in
the center of the field. It was dark and quiet, and they were in
love with each other. So they began to make love there.

Apparently by chance, three other young people happened
by, all boys. Two of them were adults by legal standards;
the third was only fifteen. They almost stumbled over the
couple.

Soon they were making fun of them, and then the matter became more serious. One of the group attacked the boy and girl,
and then the other two boys became involved. The young man
was pistol-whipped to death with a gun one of the three was
carrying. The girl, screaming, was repeatedly raped, sodomized
and subjected to other acts.

She was very ill for many months after, but she lived to re-
gain her health—and to tesify against the three, who had been
quickly arrested for their crime.

The elder two, over eighteen years of age, were tried and
convicted as adults and are now serving time in state prison.
The third, the fifteen-year-old, was tried as a minor and sent to
a youth facility to serve until age twenty-one.

And so, you might imagine, the sad story ended. But as in the
case of Jeff, Martha, and Wally, such cases seem never to end.
For the youngest finally reached the age of twenty-one and expected to be released back into society. But this was not to be.
There was such a public outcry that a trial was held to determine if he was suitable for release. Since the outcry came from
the area of the state where the crime had been committed, the
court held that a *change of venue* was in order. A change of
venue is an order that moves a trial away from an area where
the court feels that twelve disinterested jurors cannot be found.

So the trial was held in a more "neutral" area, and the jury
found that the young man was not rehabilitated and should not
be released. He is still serving his sentence.

What Happens in Juvenile Court

Most of you will never face going to juvenile court, or being tried for a serious crime. Maybe you have broken a window, cheated on an exam, crashed a party to which you weren't invited, or even shoplifted or taken money from your parents. These are serious matters, matters you will carry on your conscience for the rest of your life (whether or not you believe it now), but teenagers seldom commit grand larceny or kill anyone.

So, since we cannot say exactly what the punishment of Jeff, Martha, and Wally is going to be, let's combine the three of them into one person for the sake of going through juvenile court. Let's invent a young man named "Charley."

Charley is, generally speaking, a pretty decent guy, but he constantly skates on the very edges of purely legal behavior. Charley, who is sixteen, is the type who will look at your paper during a test, or grab a candy bar from the local store without paying, or sneak into a game rather than show his student card. Charley, whom everybody seems to like well enough, is trouble waiting to happen. He is the kind of guy you tend to hold at arm's length because you know that sooner or later he is going to fall and that when he does he will probably take with him whoever is nearby. You may have known a "Charley" (or a "Charlene") in your life.

What Happens First

Most often, the juvenile-court process begins when an officer arrests a minor. The officer can, without a warrant for the arrest, take him or her into custody though it must be for a temporary period of time. Let's say that Charley has smashed a parking meter on a side street downtown to collect the change inside, and that a couple of businessmen in nearby stores saw him do it. In a town the size of Charley's, they recognized the

"young troublemaker" and turned him in. After all, they rea-
soned, their tax money would be used to repair the meter and to
replace the money Charley stole.

So they called the police, and Officer Harkness responded.
He dropped by the school, walked into the office, and asked the
principal to summon Charley. Charley responded, though when
he saw Officer Harkness, he wished he hadn't. Officer Harkness
asked Charley to come with him, and with little choice in the
matter, Charley complied.

Off to the police station they went for questioning.

What Happens Next

In most states, the police have several choices in the handling of a juvenile who has committed a crime. But already it
has become an unpleasant matter for Charley, in spite of all the
rights guaranteed him by present-day law. The police may
question Charley, then release him. Perhaps they do not feel he
has committed the crime, or perhaps they feel that the crime,
though committed, is too minor to be worth prosecuting.

Police may also, in a town where it is available, decide to as-
sign a youth such as Charley to a sponsored community activity.
Although there may be a question as to whether or not such a
program could be of any help to Charley, many young people
are helped by being allowed to "work off their crime" in community cleanup jobs or some other community-sponsored, po-
lice-managed activity. Of course this must be done under the
supervision of the probation department so that the minor's
rights are not violated, but these *diversion programs* have
proven to be very helpful to both society and the minor in trouble.

The result of this, generally worked out between the police,
the parents, and the probation department, is a cool-off time in
which the minor has a chance to think things over and no permanent police record will be filed. Meanwhile, the community
benefits from some free labor.

If you think this is "slave" labor, you could be right, but look at the alternative.

The police might ask Charley to sign a promise to appear later, then send him home. But suppose the policeman thinks that Charley's crime is serious enough to hold him at the police department until a trial. This the officer cannot do on his own. To hold a juvenile, a court must speak. So the policeman might call in a probation officer to investigate Charley's behavior to see whether he must be held. Charley might be the type to run off if he is released or to go out and commit another crime. In this case, Charley was known to be a problem with the law. He had been in trouble before, even though it was rather minor. So, since the probation officer knows Charley's record, he has choices to make. For Charley has been turned over to him by Officer Harkness.

Mr. Williams, the probation officer, looks across the table at Charley. He could, of course, merely release Charley. He has that authority, as does Officer Harkness. Or Mr. Williams could place Charley under the supervision of the probation department. By now, of course, Charley's parents have been informed, and they may have chosen to hire a lawyer to protect Charley's rights. To this point, the lawyer cannot object to anything that has happened because so far nothing has happened to hurt Charley, to get him to confess, or to jail him.

Probably if Mr. Williams decides to place Charley under the supervision of the department, it means that Charley will have a hearing—but not necessarily before a juvenile court. If Charley's parents consent, the department may continue to supervise Charley for a period of time. The lawyer will probably agree to this because supervision would mean only that the department will watch over Charley, but not hold him. If there is to be a hearing, Charley's parents and the lawyer will be invited to attend, to give their testimony.

But suppose Mr. Williams feels that Charley's crime was serious enough to hold him in detention—and that he cannot do, any more than Officer Harkness could, without going to still another protector of Charley's legal rights.

What Happens Then

Then Charley will go through a detention hearing. It may be before a judge, usually a superior court judge assigned to hear such matters or a referee, who might be an attorney, or a skilled probation officer. This judge or referee, after hearing the facts (which are fully and completely recorded) will make a final decision on Charley's detention, but not on his alleged crime.

Although the time varies from state to state, an average time that a minor can be held in detention without a full hearing on his or her alleged crime is fifteen days. During these days the minor is held in a lockup, but it is generally in an area that is away from hardened offenders and as pleasant as possible under the circumstances. After all, to this point the minor has not been found guilty of anything.

In Charley's case, the decision was made, based on his past record, to hold him in detention until his court hearing. But most juveniles do not get this far into the system. The police and the probation department will often bend over backward to work with a problem minor, to try to get him into counseling, perhaps along with his parents, to help him get straight. This is especially true in the case of a first offender. Police and probation officials do not like to detain a first offender. Rather, they prefer to offer first offenders a chance to pay back society in some other way.

But poor Charley went off to juvenile hall. He didn't like it, not at all, but what could he do? He felt that everyone was against him and that his parents didn't really care. Well, he could handle it. It wouldn't be too bad.

And Finally

Still, it wasn't much fun to be tied down to one place, to have to come and go when others told him to come and go. Charley didn't like the room he was sleeping in, and he didn't like the idea of that lock clicking every night. What if there was a fire, he thought to himself? How could he get out? What he hated most of all was the dumb uniform he had to wear. There was no closet room for his clothes, and since no one was held long enough to need extra clothes, everybody wore the uniform of faded jeans, stenciled T-shirts, and tennis shoes.

Charley hated the tennis shoes, which were high-topped, like basketball shoes, and he was beginning to hate the whole affair. Sure, you got some time to go out and play a little ball or watch TV and the food wasn't all that bad, but Charley found himself missing his friends at school. Well, he knew he had a hearing coming up in a few days. In fact, that was one of the topics of conversation at the facility. And there were other topics, the same ones over and over again.

How long have you been here?

When is your hearing?

What are you in for?

It was big talk, Charley could see. It was talk just like in a real jail, spiced with heavy profanity and suggestions about what the speaker would do if he could just get over to the women's section. Charley knew they were girls, not women, and he was getting very tired of hearing losers brag about what they were going to do when they "got out."

But he was stuck with it for the time being. Finally, though, his hearing date arrived, and he was ready. He still had hopes that he could beat the rap. After all, this was his first serious offense. And besides, deep down he knew he didn't want to go through this again and again, as some of the others at the hall had done. If they were life's real losers, and Charley could see that some of them were, then he was only half a loser at the time. He still had a chance.

Meanwhile, Charley's parents and his lawyer had been notified in writing of the hearing date. The lawyer had been given time to work out a defense with Charley. In fact, he had spent many hours with Charley, talking to him about what he had done, and what he might want to do with his life. The lawyer wasn't, Charley had begun to realize, a bad guy at all. In fact, Charley even found himself liking Ron Hannigan.

On the morning of the hearing, everybody was in court. Charley nodded to his parents and took his place beside his attorney. It was more like a discussion among all the parties involved than a trial. But there was a court reporter present, tapping away on her machine, recording every word that was spoken.

Charley was grateful for the presence of Ron Hannigan, but he knew that according to the law, if his parents had not been able to afford to pay Hannigan, the court would have appointed and paid for a lawyer for him, to be sure Charley's rights were not violated. By the same token, if Charley did not want a lawyer, he would not *have* to have one. He could *waive* the right to counsel after talking to the judge and to his parents. Some matters are small enough that the defendant might want to just chat with the judge and his parents, and work things out that way.

Ron Hannigan had told Charley what was going to happen at this *adjudicatory hearing* (where a judgment would be made) and that the public was not allowed to attend. In fact, one man in the back of the room was asked to leave by Judge Watkins, the judge who would hear Charley's case. Most hearings regarding minors are closed hearings. The public and the press are not allowed to be there. Only Charley, his parents, his lawyer, the judge, the court reporter, the probation officer, and the district attorney (who represents "the people" in all cases in court) were there.

First Judge Watkins reminded Charley of his right to counsel, his right to present witnesses in his behalf, and to confront and cross-examine witnesses for the other side. He also told Charley again that he did not have to testify against himself or admit to anything at all.

Charley was worried and concerned, but he was impressed by the fact that everybody seemed to be protecting him. Nobody seemed to be out to "get" him, not even the probation officer or the district attorney. They had both smiled at him and seemed to be friendly and helpful. It wasn't at all like a big murder trial, where the other side really is trying to send you away.

But it was still serious business, especially to Charley, as the court clerk read the petition prepared by the probation department. The petition alleged, but did not charge, that Charley had smashed the parking meter and taken the change inside. As the clerk read the paper, Charley made a decision. He could do one of two things. He could plead innocent. Then the state would attempt to prove the case against him. The district attorney, probably represented by a deputy district attorney, would present evidence and call witnesses, including the two merchants who said they had seen Charley breaking the parking meter. These men would be sworn to tell the truth just as in any other court of law. Then Charley himself might be called to the stand if he agreed to testify. But by going to the witness stand, Charley would be permitting the district attorney to cross-examine him. He knew this could be very tough—especially since he had broken into the meter.

The court would go through all the procedures of a trial, but instead of a jury, Judge Watkins would decide the case. If he found that the allegations in the petition had not been proven, he would dismiss the case and tell Charley he was free to go. If he found the petition to be substantially correct, he would go on to the next phase of the matter.

Charley could also plead guilty. He had been doing a lot of thinking, and, after consultation with his lawyer, he asked to speak to the judge. In juvenile matters, this is fairly easy to arrange. Of course he would listen, said the judge.

"Then I would like to say, Judge Watkins, that I am guilty. I did break into the parking meter. I regret it now, but I did do it and I'm ready to get this all over with and take the consequences."

"Are you sure you know what you're saying?" asked the judge. "Did anybody tell you to plead this way? Are you speaking for yourself? You have a right to a trial, you know, a trial where you could be found not guilty."

"Yes, sir, I know what I'm saying. But too many people have spent too much time and money on this as it is—including my parents. I'd just like to get it over with."

"Do you concur with this, Mr. Hannigan?" asked the judge.

"Yes, Your Honor. My client has decided this is the best way—and I agree with him."

"Mr. and Mrs. Smith?" asked the judge of Charley's parents. They both nodded.

"Why did you decide to admit to it, Charley?" asked Judge Watkins.

"Well, I've learned a lot and seen a lot in the past few days, Your Honor. I was wrong and I'm willing to take whatever I have to take. I'd like to clear this up and get back to living my life again."

In a move not that unusual in a juvenile court matter, Judge Watkins leaned forward and spoke to Charley. "And how do *you* think I should handle this matter, Charley?"

Charley considered the judge's words. He knew from what Ron Hannigan had told him that the judge could do one of several different things. Of course he hoped that the judge wouldn't send him back to detention, but he knew that it would be logical. Charley could also be declared a ward of the court and placed on probation in a foster home, in a public or private institution, or a county "honor" ranch or a county juvenile home.

Or, in more severe cases, the judge could send the juvenile to a prisonlike youth authority farm.

"I don't know, Judge, but I can tell you that once I have served whatever you decide, I'm going to straighten out my life and do better than before." Then Charley considered for a minute. He couldn't resist. With a twinkle in his eye, he said, "One thing for sure . . . no more parking meters!"

Judge Watkins covered his smile with his hand and said, "I am going to take this under consideration while I read the social reports." In many states he would not have been permitted to read certain reports of the probation department until after the case was settled so that he would be in no way swayed by that evidence. "Meanwhile, I am going to release you to your parents' custody. You will be informed as to when to come back for final disposition. Now, this hearing is adjourned."

In Charley's case, the judge called everyone back in to his chambers a week later. He declared Charley a ward of the court for a certain period of time, but allowed him to return home for as long as he could stay free of any trouble. He required Charley to report once a week to the probation department and to attend classes in a city citizenship program every Saturday morning for eight weeks.

Finally, every Saturday afternoon for the next six months, Charley would have to contribute public service in a parks cleanup program in his town.

Does Charley Have a Record?

Yes and no. For the time being, Charley does have a court record, but in most states there is a means of sealing that record after the minor reaches the age of eighteen. Later it is even possible, if the minor has lived a life free of any criminal activity, to have the record expunged, or erased completely.

So what does Charley, after age eighteen, write on an employment application if it asks if he has a criminal record? He writes *no* because he no longer has a record. He has a clean slate. He never had a "criminal" record in the first place. Nobody can check and find out about it because the record of court proceedings is no longer there. For more about how to answer these questions, see the following chapter.

12

You *Can* Fight City Hall

The right of appeal is another right you have in juvenile court. If Charley had been found guilty instead of pleading guilty, Ron Hannigan would, or at least could, have appealed. He could have asked another court to hear the case against Charley all over again.

Appeals, in fact, are where new law is often made. It was on appeals to the U.S. Supreme Court that the cases of Kent and Gault and Winship were heard. You remember that the findings of the high court in these cases brought many new rights (and, yes, responsibilities) to teenagers.

One young man, Eric, took a car he had recently purchased to have some work done on the power steering. It was a simple job. One of the hoses in the unit had scraped against something and was leaking. Power-steering fluid was leaking out on the street, and only minutes after a fill, he would lose the power steering. He knew he had to have the hose fixed, so he went to the local dealer for his model car.

"Fifteen bucks for the hose," said the man who wrote up the service order, "and twenty bucks for labor. That'll be thirty-five dollars total estimate."

The price seemed high to Eric, but what could he do? He had to have the hose fixed or he would spend thirty-five dollars on power-steering fluid. "OK," he said, "but let me know if it is going to run into any more money. I'll wait in the customer service area." It had been difficult enough to get there right after school as it was. He didn't want to wait any longer than necessary.

"Right," the man called back as he drove Eric's car into the dim back reaches of the service area.

Eric waited for the half hour or so it took to replace the hose and finally heard his name being called from the cashier's office. He went to the window, gave his name, and received his bill. It was for forty-six dollars.

"Wait a minute," Eric protested, "the estimate was for thirty-five dollars. What is this forty-six dollar stuff?"

You've all dealt with auto-agency cashiers. "What do I know?" this one asked innocently. "All I do is take the money. You pay me forty-six dollars, and I give you your keys."

"I won't pay it," Eric stated. "The estimate was for thirty-five dollars. They told me they would let me know if it went higher than that. They didn't say anything, so I won't pay it."

Of course, the cashier could not have cared less about the matter. She simply called the service writer. He explained that they hadn't been able to find Eric when they realized that the bill would be for a little more than they anticipated. So they had gone ahead.

"But I was waiting right there in the customer service area, just where I said I would be," Eric explained.

"Sorry," the auto company employee said breezily. "If you won't pay, we'll have to take the hose off. You won't be able to drive at all then." He grinned at Eric.

"Then take it off," said Eric. "I'm not going to pay."

"Now . . . now just a minute," the man stammered. "Maybe you are right. Maybe we should have tried harder to find you. Let's split the difference."

"I'll pay thirty-five dollars, no more. I won't pay any extra at all," said Eric.

"OK . . . OK . . . thirty-five dollars, then. But I don't like it," the man said. His implication was that Eric should take his business elsewhere the next time.

Meanwhile, word spread throughout the agency. Two days later the auto agency manager called, apologized, and solicited Eric's further business.

This is a mild example of "fighting City Hall." Many minors feel they cannot take on the adult world, but they are wrong. You have learned in this book that you have the same rights as adults. You must be shown the same courtesy and charged the same prices.

Ramsey Clark, former attorney general of the United States, said, "A legal right is not what someone gives you; it's what no one can take away!"

Many adults and certainly many teenagers, are frightened by loud voices, official-looking letters, cars with signs on the sides, and statements from people who sound very authoritative.

But here's a tip. If a decision affecting you seems to you to be totally wrong after you have looked at it from all sides, whether it be a decision made by your parents, school officials, or government officials, it could very well be wrong. You are not a little child. You have long since learned right from wrong. When you know you are right, fight!

If you think you have been swindled, mistreated, or generally handled poorly by a salesclerk, a teacher, or even a parent, you don't have to lie down and take it. If the culprit is a parent, argue logically and quietly for your point of view. Don't rant and rave, but be firm and friendly. Allow your parent his or her point of view and explain yours rationally and calmly. Do the same with a teacher, and go even further, if necessary, to principal.

If you are dealing with a salesclerk or a service or repair person, keep in mind the consumer fraud units in every city. Your local police department or your local district attorney's office can direct you. You have as much right to use these agencies as an adult does. Legal-aid services will listen to any minor who complains logically and calmly.

What if there is a law, cut and dried, that you feel is a hindrance? It is a law, in your opinion, that hurts more than it helps. Fight to get the law changed. Write or visit your local or state officials or even your senator or representative. You can take local matters to your city council. Such councils listen carefully to the complaints of their constituents, even if they are youthful. If you don't vote now, you will before too long, and they know that.

You can fight City Hall and win.

If the real truth were known, City Hall is more afraid of you than you are of it. You can upset their smooth-running apple cart, and they would rather listen to you and solve your problem than have you go shouting to somebody saying that they wouldn't listen. Suppose, for example, the local newspaper got the idea that a local official wouldn't listen to you because you are young. That would be very embarrassing to him, and he knows it.

No, City Hall understands that it is better to handle a problem before it gets out of hand.

Shortly after he was elected, the mayor of one town had installed a set of fire stairs leading out of the back of his office. He must certainly have been afraid of fire, right? Wrong! He had the stairs installed so that he could "duck out the back" when his constituents came to the front door to complain. He lasted only one term.

Charley, described in Chapter 11, had a record. He hoped to get it expunged. Then he would not have to discuss it on future employment applications. But what if you have had a problem in your youth, had the record sealed, and finally expunged? What is the proper answer to the more sweeping question when it is asked on one of the many forms we all fill out:

"Have you ever been found guilty or convicted of a crime?"

The proper answer is still no. And this is true whether or not the record has been sealed or expunged. Juvenile proceedings do not result in guilty findings, nor are they criminal actions in the strict legal sense.

What Can Happen If You Do Not Remain Aware?

One young high school student, at the request of her civics teacher, was completing an assignment on extreme political groups. She wrote to one of these groups for some literature. She received the literature and incorporated it into her report.

Meanwhile, she noticed that she was being followed. Then she learned that the FBI was asking questions about her and her family. They were going around the neighborhood and asking about how the family lived, the father's credit rating, and other personal matters. Had her father ever been arrested, and how did he treat his family, and did he seem to go to meetings a lot at night?

The family complained to the local authorities, who finally informed the FBI that the family was a solid unit, good Americans, and that the girl was only doing a school assignment. Oh, fine, said the FBI. They apologized to the family, and the matter was forgotten.

But not for long. The family learned that the girl's file was still active in the "subversive connections" file at FBI headquarters. The girl sued, and finally her file was removed and destroyed. Otherwise she might have faced a real problem later in life. She might have gone for employment and had the file opened to face her. Or she might have been refused security clearance somewhere because of the file. Or she could have been denied a passport.

Always be vigilant and careful in such a situation. Fight back. People will listen to you if you fight honestly and from firm ground. Though they might discourage you from fighting the government, when you win, they will make amends and you will be free.

And that is how it is supposed to be in this country.

If You Only *Plan* a Crime

Is it a crime to plan a robbery or a murder if you do not attempt to carry it out? No, if you are all alone. If you are alone, nobody knows what you are planning, and your plan is not a crime if nothing ever comes of it.

But if you involve somebody else, anybody else, then it *is* a crime even if you never go through with it. By involving somebody else, you have made the plan a conspiracy to commit a crime, and that in itself is a crime. So don't go around asking other people to help you pull a job. If you want to dream about such weird things, dream about them alone.

Protection From Child Abuse

Everyone has heard of child abuse. This is when an adult uses a minor for illegal purposes. Maybe good old Uncle Ed likes to fondle his nieces; maybe your stepfather enjoys talking to you, his stepson, about sex, with attempted demonstrations; maybe your friendly neighbor has tried to kiss you; maybe the man down the street has raped you and you are too afraid to talk about it. Or perhaps you are being beaten or otherwise mistreated.

You have an *absolute right* not to have any of these things ever happen to you. Go to your nearest trusted adult—your parent, your teacher, your minister, your doctor—and tell him or her what is happening. Adults who do these things are ill and need help. They could eventually do even worse things if they are not helped. Remember that it will be embarrassing for them, and they may have to face treatment or even legal problems, but it will not be the end of the world for them. And it could be for some unfortunate minor they have molested.

Furthermore, it is very possible to sue for damages in cases such as this. You may be awarded damages for your emotional distress, certainly for any injuries done to you, and also for counseling to help you overcome your worries about what has happened.

Remember that child abuse also includes being beaten. Minors have an absolute right not to be battered. You don't have to take it. The law will protect you if you report it.

Statutory Rape

David and Susan have been enjoying sex with each other for some time, but then the matter is discovered by Susan's parents. Susan is a minor, but David, whom she has been dating for the past three years, has recently had a birthday and is now over the age of consent.

Susan's parents are very angry and insist that David be arrested for statutory rape.

The thing is, he *can* be. Even though they are doing nothing now they haven't been doing for years, David can now be tried as an adult rather than a juvenile. It is a much more serious matter.

Oddly though, in this day of equality and liberation, if Susan's and David's ages were reversed, Susan could only be tried for "contributing to the delinquency of a minor," not rape. The law speaks of males having "carnal knowledge" of a female, but not the opposite.

Perhaps that will change too, someday.

13

Some Last Rights and Final Words

Before you go to a lawyer, ask how the fee is set and how much it will cost you for a first appointment. You would not drive away in a car without asking how much it costs, nor would you buy an item from the supermarket wihtout knowing the cost. You wouldn't hire somebody to work for you in the yard without knowing how much he will charge. So ask the lawyer for specific details. Most lawyers charge in one of three ways.

How a Lawyer Sets His or Her Fee

Certain legal actions are very standard, and lawyers might have a fixed fee for them—making a will, for example, or handling a bankruptcy matter, or writing a lease or sales contract, or handling an uncontested divorce. In such cases a lawyer might give you a fixed fee that will cover all of his or her charges, including time in court.

Or a lawyer might work on your case by the hour, which can mean by the minute since most lawyers break down their time into segments of an hour rather than full hours. Depending on the lawyer, fees may range from as low as $35 per hour to as high as $250 per hour and even more. This can add up, especially if you develop the costly habit of telephoning your lawyer for every little thing. In this modern computerized age, every phone call goes on the record and into the books, even one that lasts only two or three minutes. So when you do call your lawyer, don't chitchat or get involved in small talk. Get down to business. His or her time is valuable (you are paying for it) and so is yours.

It is also very possible that a lawyer will take your case on a *contingency* basis. This agreement means that the lawyer doesn't get any fee at all if you don't win. Lawyers are happy to take such cases; they are usually cases that involve personal injury. Most lawyers will work for about one-third of the amount recovered if the case is settled out of court—more if the lawyer has to spend time in court. In most states you will also be responsible for all costs and expenses. Sometimes a lawyer will accept a case on a contingency basis but will require a retainer to cover some of the legal work. Usually this retainer is refunded from the proceeds of any amounts recovered.

When you or your parents need a lawyer, don't panic. If you have an accident and break your leg, you need a doctor right now. But most legal matters, even most legal emergencies, will hold for a few hours. They will hold long enough for you to seek out the best lawyer for your case.

And remember, you can dismiss a lawyer from your case any time you feel he or she is not doing the best job of handling the matter. In most states this must be done in writing (and generally speaking no other lawyer will talk to you in any detail as long as another lawyer is on the job) but it can be done, and is done frequently.

How To Find a Lawyer

The best way to find a lawyer is to ask friends and neighbors whom they have used for their legal matters in town. Lawyers work hard to develop a good reputation in whatever fields they handle, and they pride themselves on word-of-mouth recommendations from former clients. You will probably want either a family lawyer or a lawyer specializing in criminal law. If your friend or neighbor was pleased with the way a certain lawyer handled a similar case, you should be safe in going to him or her for yours. But you must work out the details, describe the case, and ascertain the fees in an initial interview. Then, if you are satisfied, retain the lawyer. If not, look elsewhere.

There are lawyer referral services in most towns. By calling a telephone number you can get the names of two of three lawyers to contact. But that is all, and the referral service will not recommend or even comment on the skill of the lawyers they are naming. They only know that these particular lawyers work in the field of law that you need.

How did they get the lawyers' names? Town lawyers pay to be listed in the lawyer referral service.

After you have received the names, you can call one of the lawyers and make an appointment. On the telephone, the lawyer will tell you how much the initial visit will cost, and it could be somewhat lower because you got his or her name through the referral service. The first short visit to describe your case may even be free. Ask to be sure. Lawyers are not offended by potential clients who discuss specific fees. On the contrary, they feel confident they will be paid by people who ask about fees at the beginning.

If you or your parents cannot afford a lawyer, there may be some type of legal assistance agency in your town. You may be eligible for free legal advice from a private attorney donating some of his or her time to community service. Or you may be able to find a very low fee arrangement. In criminal matters, you may also be represented at no charge by the public defender's office in your town. Many of these public lawyers are tenacious in their effort to represent their client in the best possible way. Also, check the list of organizations providing legal services at the end of this book.

Some Free Legal Advice for Minors

Never resist arrest, no matter how sure you are of your own innocence or how unreasonable you feel the police are being. They are not responsible, fortunately, for deciding whether or not you are guilty, and they can legally arrest you if they think you are guilty. Meanwhile, resisting arrest is a crime in itself.

If you are arrested or detained by the police, don't answer any questions, no matter how reasonable they are being, until you have a lawyer or at least until your parents are present. Simply refuse to answer: a right they know you have even if they don't like it very much.

If you have been arrested for what would be considered a felony in adult court, and this includes some shoplifting offenses and the possession of most controlled substances, ask for a lawyer before you do anything else. If you have only been joyriding in somebody else's car, a grand theft matter in adult court, ask for a lawyer. If they get you one, fine. Take his or her advice. If they don't, you have established grounds for appeal of any conviction.

If a police officer comes to your home while you are alone and asks to "look around inside" (search), be polite but tell him or her it will have to wait until your parents get home. If you allow an officer to come in, you weaken any later legal stand your parents' lawyer might take, though it still might be possible for a lawyer to get any evidence so obtained thrown out of court. But you can legally refuse to allow a police officer to come in. This is true also if you are baby-sitting in somebody else's home. If you are alone, don't permit an officer to enter. If an officer enters over your objections, that action will substantially weaken any case he or she is trying to build against you or your parents.

Your parents are going to get very angry with you if you confess to them that you have been breaking the law. If you tell them you have been shoplifting or using dope or stealing cars or even cheating in school, they are going to be very upset. They have a right to be. They often want more for you than they want for themselves. They will often give up things for themselves so that you can have something. So they will certainly be upset. But the situation, though difficult, will not be nearly as bad as if you were caught and taken to the police station. Don't be so afraid of your parents' reaction that you face such a situation alone.

Miranda v. *Arizona*

Have you ever wondered why, when a person is arrested, the police say something like this: "You have the right to remain silent. Anything you say can and will be used against you in court. You have the right to have a lawyer present during questioning. If you cannot afford a lawyer, one will be appointed for you, and you will not be questioned until your attorney is present. Do you understand these rights?"

Ernesto Miranda was arrested for kidnapping and rape. He was taken to the police station and questioned over and over again about the crime. He was not told that he could have a free lawyer, nor that he did not have to answer any questions without his lawyer's presence. He was convicted of the crimes, but in 1966 the Supreme Court overturned the conviction based on the grounds that a defendant must be told of his rights before questioning. The police do not have the right to assume you know and understand your rights. They must tell you.

One last thought on the *Miranda* decision. Often the police will ask a person they have arrested to waive these Miranda rights, to go ahead and talk even though they know they can have a lawyer present. Under almost any circumstance, even the situation where you are completely innocent and think you can prove it, it is a bad idea to waive these rights. The matter will hold until a lawyer gets there, and you can tell the lawyer your story. He will advise you how to answer the police.

Hold on to the rights you have, even if the police act angry with you. They are not your judge and jury, but only the ones who arrested you.

In the case of Miranda and many other such cases, the law was changed by the Supreme Court. Of course, the futures of these defendants are still in the hands of the courts. Often, because certain evidence can no longer be admitted at trial, the case is dismissed and the person is released on the spot. But sometimes other charges are pending against these people, and they must remain in custody. Sometimes certain charges against them are reduced because certain evidence can no longer be used and so they are returned to prison with shorter sentences for a lesser crime.

In any case, this is the system we use, and it has proven to be the best system of all. Our society has chosen to go to extremes to protect the rights of accused people. Yes, sometimes a guilty person is set free, but our society believes that mistake is much better than ever sending an innocent person to prison.

As a result of this belief, you have many rights. You have all of the rights described in this book, and nobody can take them from you.

Don't take advantage of them and always remember your responsibilities. But use your rights to their fullest when necessary.

Understand Some Terms

"The validity of the *donatio mortis causa* will withstand the attack of the intestate heirs."

Although times are changing, some lawyers still talk this way. What the lawyer meant to say, and what more and more modern lawyers are saying instead, is, in this case, "The gift given by the deceased person who was worried about his own death will be valid even though he died without a will and his heirs are fighting it."

Or how about this? "You can appear before the court in propria persona or try to find legal counsel to represent you pro bono." This means, "You can represent yourself in court or try to find a lawyer to represent you for free."

Here are some common terms to help you understand the complex world of the law.

abortion   Causing the delivery of an undeveloped human embryo or fetus in an attempt to prevent live birth.

accessory   One who contributes to or aids in the commission of a crime or who later helps to conceal the crime or the criminal.

accomplice   One who joins with the main offender in the commission of a crime.

acquit   To set free a person who has been found innocent of a crime he has been charged with.

allege   To assert or declare, to charge.

appellant   One who takes an appeal to a higher court.

bail   Security, usually a bond, cash, or property, for the temporary release of a prisoner from jail.

beyond a reasonable doubt   A judge or jury must be convinced to a "moral certainty" that the charges against a defendant are true before they can convict that person. The proof offered in the case must eliminate not all possible doubts but all reasonable doubts in a person's mind. This standard is used only in criminal proceedings, and a jury verdict must be unanimous among all jurors.

bribery   An illegal payment to a public official to influence any act, decision, vote, opinion, or other proceeding by that official.

civil case   A lawsuit involving private rights. This could be medical malpractice, divorce, or personal injury. Both parties are represented by private attorneys. This is as opposed to a criminal case, where it is the defendant—the one charged with the crime—against the people, who will be represented by a district attorney paid for by your taxes.

civil disobedience   Deliberate violation of the law for the purpose of attracting attention to a situation or to an allegedly unjust law.

class action   A lawsuit brought by one or more persons on behalf of themselves and all other persons who have suffered the same type of harm.

common law   This is the unwritten law inherited from England

and then enlarged and changed by our own courts, a body of court decisions declaring what the law is. The principle that one is innocent until proven guilty beyond a reasonable doubt is derived from common law.

conscientious objector A person who is opposed to participation in a war.

conspiracy Planning by two or more persons to commit an illegal act.

contempt of court Willful disregard of the authority of a judge or a court.

damages The amount of losses suffered by an injured party; the amount of money paid to an injured party in compensation for his injuries.

defendant The person or party against whom a suit is brought. The person accused of committing the crime.

deposition The written and sworn testimony of a witness taken outside of court.

entrapment An act of the police in inducing somebody who would not be predisposed to do such an act to commit a crime so that he or she can be convicted of doing it.

felon One convicted of committing a felony.

felony Any of various offenses, such as murder, burglary, etc., of graver character than those called misdemeanors, especially those commonly punished in the United States by imprisonment for more than a year.

fraud An illegal practice designed to deprive another person of money or property.

habeas corpus From ancient law and literally meaning "you may have the body." This demands that one who has a person in custody justify holding that person and bringing that person before a court.

hearsay evidence An out-of-court statement which is used to prove the truth of the matter stated. This kind of evidence is usually not admissible in court.

homicide The killing of another human being.

injunction An order of a court that requires or prohibits a certain action.

jury A group of people seated according to the law to hear and make a judgment in a civil or criminal case.

liable Chargeable, responsible, subject to another's enforcing an obligation against one.

libel A written or otherwise permanently published or recorded untruth about a living person.

litigant A party to a lawsuit.

manslaughter The killing of another human being without malice.

misdemeanor A violation of the law other than a felony, a relatively minor matter calling for a penalty of no more than one year in jail.

moral turpitude Contrary to good morals, contrary to honesty, modesty, or justice.

murder The killing of a human being with malice.

nolo contendere A plea of no contest in a criminal proceeding. Equivalent to a guilty plea. The defendant will not be tried and the court will impose sentence, but the defendant does not have a guilty plea on his record in case of later civil suit.

obstructing justice Any act that delays or prohibits the administration of justice.

perjury Making a false statement under oath.

plaintiff The person who is bringing the action, the person who files the lawsuit.

preponderance of evidence Evidence presented by one side, which has more probability of being true than the evidence of the other side.—A mere 51 percent is enough.

probation Allowing a person convicted of a crime to go free under supervision as long as his behavior is good.

rape Sexual intercourse with a woman without her consent.

slander False oral statements that injure the reputation of another.

statute A written law, an act of a legislature.

statutory rape Sexual intercourse by a man over the age of consent with a female under the age of consent.

summons   A written notice to appear in court or file an answer, or face loss of the suit.

test case   A case deliberately brought to court by an intentional violation of a law one does not believe in.

verdict   The finding of a jury.

warrant   A legal document from a judge, directing an officer to perform an act.

witness   A person who observes an event; a person who appears in court to testify under oath about a legal matter.

writ   A legal document or court order requiring some action.

If You Need Help

There are organizations that will help with legal defense in matters of the rights of citizens. One of the most noted of these is the American Civil Liberties Union, but there are others. Here are some addresses and names of persons to contact if you think you need help:

American-Arab Anti-Discrimination Committee
1300 Nineteenth Street NW
Washington, D.C. 20036
Don Crate, Chapter Coordinator

American Civil Liberties Union
Student's Rights Project
600 Pennsylvania Avenue SE
Washington, D.C. 20003
John Shattuck, Director, Legislative Office

Anti-Defamation League of B'nai B'rith
1640 Rhode Island Avenue NW
Washington, D.C. 20036
David A. Brody, Director

Center for National Policy Review
c/o Catholic University of America Law School
620 Michigan Avenue NE
Washington, D.C. 20064
William L. Taylor, Director

Lawyer's Committee for Civil Rights Under Law
733 Fifteenth Street NW
Washington, D.C. 20005
William L. Robinson, Director

Leadership Conference on Civil Rights
2027 Massachusetts Avenue NW
Washington, D.C. 20036
Ralph G. Neas, Executive Director

National Association for the Advancement of Colored People
Legal Defense and Educational Fund
806 Fifteenth Street NW
Washington, D.C. 20005
Phyllis McClure, Deputy Director

National Urban Coalition
1201 Connecticut Avenue NW
Washington, D.C. 20036
M. Carl Holman, President

Potomac Institute
1501 Eighteenth Street NW
Washington, D.C. 20036
Harold C. Fleming, President

Trial Lawyers for Public Justice
2000 P Street NW
Washington, D.C. 20036
Anthony Z. Roisman, Executive Director

Index

About
the Authors

ROSS R. OLNEY is the author of many books for young people, including *They Said It Couldn't Be Done*, *Modern Racing Cars*, and *Offshore!*

He says, "We have long felt that a book on legal rights is necessary, and in fact, one of the reasons my wife attended law school was so that we might write it. We have three sons who often needed to know their rights but had nowhere to go to learn of them unless they wanted to either hire an attorney or plow through rather boring legal books."

PATRICIA J. OLNEY is a practicing attorney and partner in a law firm which concentrates on the fields of personal injury, family law, contract drafting and negotiation, and business matters.

She is also the coauthor, with her husband, Ross R. Olney, of *Keeping Insects as Pets*, *Calculator Fun and Games* (both Franklin Watts), *Easy To Make Magic* (Harvey House), and *Magic* (Western). The Olneys live in Ventura, California.

WATERLOO HIGH SCHOOL LIBRARY
1464 INDUSTRY RD.
ATWATER, OHIO 44201

M
D
(

Up against the law
Olney, Ross R.

12201
347.306 Oln